The Mechanics of Falling

AND OTHER STORIES

WEST WORD FICTION

The Mechanics of falling

AND OTHER STORIES

Catherine Brady

UNIVERSITY OF

NEVADA PRESS

RENO AND

LAS VEGAS

WEST   WORD   FICTION

University of Nevada Press, Reno, Nevada 89557 USA
Manufactured in the United States of America
Design by Kathleen Szawiola

Library of Congress Cataloging-in-Publication Data
Brady, Catherine   .
The mechanics of falling and other stories / Catherine Brady.
    p.   cm. — (West word fiction series)
ISBN 978-0-87417-763-3 (alk. paper)
 I. Title.
PS3552.R2375M43 2009
 813'.54—dc22   2008041133

The paper used in this book is a recycled stock made from 30 percent post-
consumer waste materials, certified by FSC, and meets the requirements of
American National Standard for Information Sciences—Permanence of
Paper for Printed Library Materials, ANSI/NISO Z39.48-1992 (R2002).
Binding materials were selected for strength and durability.

FIRST PRINTING
18 17 16 15 14 13 12 11 10 09
5 4 3 2 1

Oh, for this new pure life to begin, when one could go straight forward, looking one's fate boldly in the eyes, confident that one was in the right, could be gay and free! This life was bound to come sooner or later.

ANTON CHEKHOV, "The Betrothed"

Contents

ACKNOWLEDGMENTS   XI

LOOKING FOR A FEMALE TENET   I

THE DAZZLING WORLD   20

SLENDER LITTLE THING   42

SCISSORS, PAPER, ROCK   63

THE MECHANICS OF FALLING   86

LAST OF THE TRUE BELIEVERS   106

WAIT FOR INSTRUCTIONS   130

MUCH HAVE I TRAVELED   150

SEVEN REMEDIES   170

THOSE WHO WALK DURING THE DAY   191

WICKED STEPMOTHER   208

Acknowledgments

I owe the greatest debt to Steven Kahn for being the best of all readers, sympathetic and tenaciously exacting. I am grateful to my literary agent, Caron Knauer, whose commitment to this manuscript never flagged, and to Margaret Dalrymple, my editor at the University of Nevada Press, who has been so encouraging every step of the way. For their boisterous moral support and generous feedback on these stories, I have promised to thank the members of my writing group in capital letters: ELIZABETH COSTELLO, JOHN VLAHIDES, DAVID BOOTH, and KARL SOEHNLEIN. Nina Schuyler and Laura Mason also graciously commented on several stories. As a writer I've gained in countless ways from my colleagues and my students in the MFA in Writing Program at the University of San Francisco—a miraculous community. Special thanks go to Pamela Blotner for her Broken Ark series of watercolors, inspiration for "Wicked Stepmother"; to D. A. Powell for all he's shared about getting the words right; to Lewis Buzbee for being a great sounding board; to Toni Graham for helpful editorial advice; and to Aaron Shurin for the *big* fun of debating over sentences. Last but not least, thanks to David and Sarah Kahn, just because.

Previous incarnations of these stories appeared in the following publications:

"Last of the True Believers" in the *Clackamas Literary Review*
(fall/winter 2000) in very different form
"Seven Remedies" in the *Kenyon Review* (fall 2004)
"The Mechanics of Falling" in the *Ontario Review*
(fall/winter 2005–6)
"Slender Little Thing" in *Other Voices* (spring/summer 2006)
"Those Who Walk During the Day" in *Cimarron Review*
(winter 2007)

The Mechanics of Falling

AND OTHER STORIES

Looking for a female Tenet

The first night they thought about going home. But Jules and Mary Lee told themselves there was a finite limit on their time in hell. Jules had gotten them the summer job by writing in answer to an ad—easy hours waitressing at a rustic lodge, free room and board in the beautiful foothills of the Sierra Nevada—and as soon as they were shown to the room they were expected to share, they understood their mistake. The room was in a hall off the restaurant kitchen and smelled of grease from the cooking vents, effluence that had bubbled and stained the wallpaper, and the bare mattresses on the cots looked as if they'd been stuffed with straw and carelessly sewn up. Mary Lee checked the bathroom: a rust-stained sink and a toilet ringed with grime and no shower.

But to turn around and go back. Mary Lee would have had to return to her parents' house with her five brothers and sisters, share a room with her older sister who was working as a bank teller and still fighting with the younger kids for her spot on the sofa. Jules had just the one older brother and a sprawling suburban home, but she would not live under her parents' roof.

Beating dust from the mattresses, Jules said that a summer with their families, this last summer before they graduated from Stanford and were completely free, also meant doing hard time.

They keep their house cold as hell in summer, my parents, Jules said. Three months of my mother asking me please not to raise my voice. Singing out my name whenever she wants me. Joo-lee. And wanting to know when she's going to see the benefits of my expensive education. She's got the whole country on her side now. Reagan's in the White House, smiling away. Everyone else is cheerful.

I get it, Mary Lee said. Worse hell.

That was the deal. Jules believed *her*. Mary Lee had shed the shame she felt in high school, wanting no one to see that house she came from, cramped as the belly of a ship, listing with every grievance of her father's—and so many had flared for so long that even he forgot why—and had learned to tell it as if it were more awful than it was, gauge of how far, how fast she had come. She'd marshaled her story even if she wasn't sure how to brush off what else clung to her, like grains of sand to damp skin: the feeling of being wholly owned by a mother who buttoned you into blouses and licked her thumb to press your eyebrows flat; the pleasure of devouring bread fried in Crisco and sprinkled with sugar, a treat; the reflex of cringing at the nearness of a father who'd smack you as quick as he would any of the others, not bother to single anyone out.

Standing in the room Jules could shrug off as no worse than what she'd face at home, Mary Lee heard her father, expecting from his children what he did not expect from himself when he was thwarted: No use crying over spilt milk.

At the beautiful resort the parched mountains glared with

reflected sunlight; the sky did not change from one day to the next; the lodge was musty and dark inside; and most of their customers came from the adjacent campground, where the stammering noise of TVs and radios floated from campers and tents all day long. Jules and Mary Lee worked two shifts, from twelve to two and from six to midnight. In summer the manager kept the bar open late and hired a rock band, which drew locals too, young men from the ranches in the foothills who wore cowboy hats, girls who dressed in too-tight jeans and ringleted their hair around a curling iron. It was true, what the manager had written to Jules, that here you could go out at night and see a sky you'd never glimpse in the city, oppressively populated, afflicted with a rash of dim stars.

Jules had a car, her parents' old Ford sedan; they would get away on their days off. They rolled out of bed at eleven and put on their waitress uniforms, peach cotton dresses that buttoned up the front and little white aprons. The dresses had darts at the waist to give them an hourglass shape that Jules filled out but Mary Lee did not. They entered the blissfully air-conditioned restaurant at eleven thirty to swill coffee before helping Ginny, the real waitress, whose years on her feet had left her with a grim face and a body disconcertingly lean and supple. On the question of their competence, Ginny seemed indifferent; the most fellow feeling she could muster was the occasional muttered epithet *cockaroach* when one of the customers, hers or theirs, behaved badly. At two o'clock Jules and Mary Lee took off their aprons and left Ginny on her own. Sometimes they swam in the pool behind the lodge, but more often they lay on their nun-like beds and read. At six Mary Lee and Jules returned to the restaurant to work the dinner rush, and then, after Ginny left at eight, they served drinks and an occasional hamburger to anyone who showed up to hear the band. It was never all that crowded. They could chat behind the counter or sometimes dance with each other on the tiny dance floor.

Their room was hot at night, and mosquitoes got in through the shredded window screen. Mary Lee was pure Irish, though you had to go back two generations to find anyone in her family who had dared to cross an ocean, and she had the Irish allergic reaction to mosquito bites. Between the heat and the whine of insects, she couldn't sleep. She was ashamed to be so bothered when Jules slept fine. In the first week, when they thought they could make some money off tips, Ginny posted a note on the corkboard by the cash register: *looking for a female tenet, quite and friendly.* Jules asked about the room for rent, tried to cajole Ginny into letting her and Mary Lee share it for the summer. Ginny tapped sugar packets into a neat row in a dispenser. You're not Christians, she said.

They couldn't have afforded the rent anyway. The people from the campground rarely left more than a dollar on the table, and the locals counted out tips in coins that weighted Mary Lee's pockets by the end of her shift, and even at night when most of their customers were drunk they did not forget to be parsimonious. One night as Mary Lee and Jules sat on their beds, counting out the change they'd spilled from the deep pockets of their uniforms, Mary Lee began to cry. She had calculated the minimum she needed to make in order to afford to go back to school, and at this rate she'd fall short.

Jules said, That's the hold your working-class background has on you. Everything won't get taken away from you in one fell swoop. Don't panic.

At the end of every semester Jules woke to the fact that she might not pass her courses, pulled all-nighters to write papers, crammed desperately in the library, took cold showers to force her mind to alertness. Mary Lee maintained a straight-a average at an unwavering pace.

She said, I can't afford to panic.

Jules waved a hand. That doesn't always make you one up on me.

Jules and Mary Lee had met in an art history class last year. Jules had wanted Mary Lee to teach her the trick of discerning which facts they'd be expected to spit out on a test, as if the slide shows and field trips to art galleries were aimed at this winnowing. So Mary Lee talked to Jules about Giotto and Masaccio—not on the course list—and how van Gogh could make her cry, and Jules got it: once you knew you could, you spent the fortune amassed in those facts, recklessly. In this realm Mary Lee did not have it in her to knuckle under. She was quick to suggest the emperor had no clothes when their professor took the class to an exhibit of photographs, women's crotches shot from every conceivable angle. Ugly. Obscene. Feminist statement, my ass, she'd protested to Jules. But Jules said it was fantastic, the way the photographs refused to eroticize female genitals and activated discomfort. This time it was Mary Lee who needed instruction, who studied the photographs again, the yoke of her modest Irish mother around her neck.

If Jules did not make the expected weekly phone call to her parents, Mary Lee wrote to her mother every Sunday after they finished the lunch shift. She commiserated with her mother about her surreptitious nighttime trips to stuff garbage bags in trash cans on street corners because her father had decided the city had no right, *no right*, to charge for trash collection before the service was provided. She described the blue jay she and Jules had inadvertently taught to screech at their window every morning by feeding it cracker crumbs, and she added a line about the stars at night, the as-advertised stars.

When they swept aside their fistfuls of change that night, Jules promised, Summer's not over yet. She cut the shoulder pads from a shirt and stuffed them in her bra, and when it improved her take, she made Mary Lee do the same. The men in shorts who came in with a wife and bickering kids were the most likely to reward flirtation. The ranchers went for a combination of wide-eyed innocence and pinned-up hems. And if Mary Lee and Jules served up a Coke or a side order of fries and didn't charge for it, a few extra quarters would be left on the table by every person who believed he'd gotten away with something. The two of them made only a few more dollars a week, but that came to be beside the point.

Their afternoon breaks took the shape of ritual. If Mary Lee had to wait for a table to pay the check before she could finish her lunch shift, she bitterly resented every minute of lost time. With no one to care what they did to the walls of their room, Jules had nailed up a couple of cheap bedspreads to hide the wallpaper. It was so hot they shed their uniforms and lay on their beds in T-shirts and underwear, reading and drinking iced coffee and listening to music on the stereo Jules had packed into her car, Miles Davis's *Sketches of Spain*, Bill Evans, Ella Fitzgerald singing "April in Paris." Mary Lee was working her way through all of Faulkner. Jules was reading Borges, squinting as smoke from her cigarette curled around her face. Now and then they would read a paragraph or two out loud to one another, erotic pleasure that ruffled the stillness of afternoon heat. For those four hours every day their lives were nothing but fallow indulgence.

Then they started to hang out with the band. Four guys living in an RV at the campground, and they came in just before they were slated to play, ordering as much free food as they could eat, as desperate as Jules and Mary Lee to stretch their income from this gig. Jules and Mary Lee hovered at their table to talk. Jules said, One, they'll have weed. Two, maybe they'll mistake us for groupies.

The drummer stayed at the table when the girls went outside with Colin, Bert, and Joey to smoke a joint in the woods that edged the parking lot. The three of them were in their early twenties, inclined to talk about getting high when they were getting high and to speak to one another in phrases that stalled out before they could become sentences. When they talked about music in their hesitant way, Bert and Joey deferred to Colin, the lead singer. Their shirt collars always curled under and their jeans looked soiled, and Mary Lee tried not to blame them—they had to cart laundry to the single washer and dryer at the lodge, and first accumulate the correct change—but she could never have singled out one of them the way Jules did Colin.

They came back inside to find Owen still at the table, a shot glass engulfed by his long, broad-tipped fingers. He was older than the others, his face taut and creased, so tall he had to slouch in his chair to keep his knees from banging the table. He claimed he was the only black man within a radius of ten miles. What am I doing here? he said. I can't walk through the campgrounds alone at night.

At first he didn't say much to Jules or Mary Lee. He watched them and smiled knowingly. Two little college girls. Two smart little college girls. You about as rare out here as I am.

When Owen decided to talk to them, he argued with Mary Lee about Frantz Fanon—first he had to praise her for knowing who Fanon was—and sighed over Jules's taste in music. Miles, he said, had his moments, but he'd taken jazz in a shabby direction. Owen would loan her a few records, Sidney Bechet and, yeah, Ornette Coleman; Jules would have to learn to like him if she had any self-respect. And you're the expert on that? Jules said, and Owen grinned as if she'd given in: You'll figure that out for yourself, won't you. The other guys would tease Owen (rave on!) and then peter off into silence when he harangued Mary Lee and Jules about what his bandmates were too dumb to register, standing there with their mouths open waiting for the one drop that might fall, *trickle-down economics my ass*, and the flow of his talk was studded with compliments—*don't need to tell that to a smart girl like you.* He touched Mary Lee when he talked to her, flirtatious taps on the wrist or the shoulder, and once he fingered the pinned-up hem of her dress and promised to loan her a needle and thread while his warm hand lingered on her thigh.

When the bartender came over to the table to tell Jules and Mary Lee to wait on their customers, as he eventually always had to do, Owen laughed and told them they'd better step smart now.

At night in their room, with a small fan to stir the air and drown out the buzz of the mosquitoes, Jules and Mary Lee reconnoitered like guerrillas bent on harassing an army hampered by its size and its presumption of advantage. Jules curled up on Mary Lee's bed to retail her first sexual encounter with Colin: on a blanket in the woods he had pawed her like a dog digging in dirt. Which made Jules think of the wrong thing, that the band was aptly named, and what was Owen doing cycling through places like this with the Dharma Dogs?

You'll figure that out for yourself, won't you, Mary Lee said.

Jules made a face. I can't even tell if Colin's too dumb to know better or if he was just trying to get off easy.

Don't let *that* happen.

Jules pulled Mary Lee's arm over her shoulder. I didn't want to spoil it for him by giving instructions.

Aw, shit, that was so female. Aw, shit, it was like coming to rest to end up here again, mired in some squishy substrata of feelings. Too tempting. Until last spring Mary Lee had only nursed unrequited crushes on boys more beautiful, more *something* than she was. Jules had said, just go get one, and hunkered down inside that borrowed luck, Mary Lee managed to wheedle a drunken boy into bed, to crow over it with Jules afterward. How was that possible, to be pleased she'd bagged him and then, when Monty didn't call her again, to suffer in the same way as before? But Jules was there to listen and console.

A few days after he'd inspected the hem of her uniform, Owen knocked at the door of their room where no one ever came. Jules had gone to the pool to use the gritty communal shower, but Mary Lee preferred to stay in and read when she got off at two. She had shed her uniform, pulled the shoulder pads from her bra and set them on the windowsill to dry in the hot air. Before answering the door, she wriggled into a T-shirt and shorts.

Owen looked around the room. Damn. They keep you worse than they do us.

He had come to sew her dress. Though his cookie tin made

a makeshift sewing kit, its contents were arranged in gorgeous order, spools arrayed on the perimeter, tight rolls of basting ribbon and measuring tape wedged in among them, a velvety pincushion at the center, punctured by an array of needles and blue-tipped pins. He even had sewing scissors sheathed in a red leather case.

He sat cross-legged on her bed to sew the dress and had her sit beside him so he could teach her a thing or two. How to knot a thread by looping it around a finger and tugging. How to avoid puckering fabric when you took a stitch. He stitched meticulous tiny *x*'s of thread, evenly spaced, looping the needle in the air with rhythmic accuracy. Drumming, he used the fulcrum of his wrist in the same way, and even when speed blurred his hands he seemed rooted in stillness.

Mary Lee had known not to react when he rested his hand on her thigh. Tests were easy. But her self-possession was pricked by his proximity, the long bones of his fingers, the duskiness of his bare feet tucked under his calves, the span of his shoulders, the way he used his flexible wrist. No, not pricked but split: some beautiful impulse unspooling from a body inadequate to it, bony and deficient. She wasn't some frightened virgin. She'd disposed of that, so easily: instinct had told her just how to bracket that boy with her hips, even if Monty was so drunk he had to ask her not to move so much.

About to rethread the needle, Owen nudged the book she had left open on the bedspread. What a good girl, improving your mind on your own time. What college you go to anyway?

Stanford.

La dee dah.

It's practically free, she said. I got a better scholarship deal than I could have gotten at the state university. My father's a forklift operator.

Those your credentials? He grinned. You trying to make me feel safe with you?

Again her shame was acutely physical. Her puny bony self.

It took a long time to sew a hem by hand.

When Owen finished, he traced the line of stitches, nearly invisible, even as teeth, no more possible than the blur of his hands drumming. He was sorry he hadn't creased the hem with an iron before he began.

He said, My wife can't sew worth shit. And she thinks you only have to press the cuffs and collar to make a shirt presentable.

Another grin to warn her what was coming. But she's good at other things.

What wife? Where? What did she do while he drove up and down the state in an RV with those boys? What a man might teach you was nothing like what you might learn from another woman, nothing like Mary Lee's routine with Jules in which abjection was intimacy. Owen packed up his sewing kit and departed without touching her.

Jules and Mary Lee began to spend their days off with the guys from the band, driving up to the national park in the mountains to hike, boating on a lake, taking in a livestock fair. This was a version of the summer they had been promised. They drove out to a stable to take a trail ride together, Colin sitting in front with Jules and reading aloud the billboards along the road, posted like place-names for this foreign terrain—3 MI. TO DREISER'S FARM STAND, ABORTION IS MURDER, CHRIST THE LORD IS RISEN. Owen poked Jules: That's what you get for teaching him how to read. Jules said, Yeah, he rewards all my efforts, and Colin fanned his hand over hers, as if he knew some secret route past this contempt. He must have, because in their room at night Jules would confide hoarsely to Mary Lee that he'd spent an hour of her afternoon break setting ice cubes on her belly, teaching her not to shiver until the ice had melted.

Mary Lee had wanted to ride horseback in the mountains, imagining something like flight, gliding across a meadow at a gallop, but the trail horses were irritable, beaten-down creatures who plodded after one another and nipped whenever another horse got too close. Owen knew how to ride—yet another area of expertise—but even he couldn't spur his horse to trot for more than a few yards. Mary Lee was grateful her horse could not be prodded to life. With every step the horse took, she listed jerkily to one side or the other, couldn't overcome the sensation that she would fall from that unstable perch.

Mary Lee said no the next time Jules wanted to go for a trail ride. She said no when Jules thought they had enough time between two and six to drive out to a lake for a swim. She did not go along when Jules and Colin devoted a day off to a trip to Bakersfield, the nearest real town, to score weed. Nearly every afternoon Colin and Jules split a fat joint, and Jules would mimic his hazy speech till he flared into anger, or amuse herself by repeating a phrase of his with exaggerated indolence. Jules complained that Mary Lee was resigning herself for the duration instead of having fun. But each trail ride cost twenty dollars Mary Lee would need in the fall, and she had no trouble weighing the pleasure of hours of reading against an afternoon with Colin and Jules.

Owen sometimes loaned Mary Lee books to read. He never came to the room again, but he began to come to the restaurant in the afternoon, at a time when Ginny was refilling ketchup bottles for the dinner service and he could keep a table for several hours. Ginny never rushed when they were busy and never just stood at the counter when things were slow. She could use up fifteen minutes transferring a few tablespoons of ketchup from a nearly empty bottle to a full one. Her equilibrium remained intact even when Jules badgered her about the notice yellowing on the bulletin board—Come on, it would be like a slumber party. I'm in no hurry, Ginny would answer. If Owen sat at one of her tables, Ginny would calmly slap the check on the table when he told her she was looking fine today. If he sat at one of Jules's tables and said even one thing about the stupid peach dress, Jules would answer wearily, Oh, Owen, put up or shut up. She didn't know how Mary Lee could tolerate Owen's bullshit. It's pro forma with him, Mary Lee said. He's just . . . filling the bill and then laughing up his sleeve. Jules rolled her eyes and said, Where's the gain in that? Mary Lee did not ask where was the gain in Colin's fistful of ice cubes.

When Owen sat at one of Mary Lee's tables, she would linger when she came to refill his coffee cup, compelled by the flattery embedded in the flow of his talk, current that snatched up whatever came in its path, as if his mind might run out of things to collect and disseminate. If she protested some line of his—Oh, Owen, echoing Jules—he'd shake his head. What screws up smart girls like you, he'd say, is you're pissed that you like it. You think you gotta protect your thinking self. Be a broad or a brain. That's the mind-body split. That goes all the way back to Augustine. And you know why men came up with philosophy and religion in the first place? So women wouldn't catch on how much of their piss-poor thinking comes from their dick.

I'm not going to fall for that either, Mary Lee said. The perfect excuse.

Owen tapped his temple and said, Sex is mostly up here, and that's your advantage, if you learn how to use it.

She was greedy for this game in which they debated as equals. They could both of them watch her blush if he admired her legs, both of them stand back and shake their heads and coax, come on, honey.

Jules was nearly always high when they started their evening shift now. Goes down easier this way, she said. It had become hard for Mary Lee to tell whether Jules was angling for a tip or something else when she chatted with a table of local guys, called each of them cowboy, tried on one of the hats they'd set on the table, or asked about those big oval belt buckles a lot of them wore, won in a rodeo or a cutting-horse competition. Cutting horse? she'd repeat slowly, with the exaggerated awe that mystified Colin. When the ranchers took off their hats they always tugged at the crown to set the crease, and it was hard to imagine them as anything but innocent creatures, entirely different from these groups of guys who drove up with fishing gear but spent most of their time holed up in a camper or some motel room off the highway, drinking. The fishing buddies could be trouble—something Mary Lee couldn't quite imagine here, where kids ran loose and every evening they showed old movies in the lodge—stiffing you for a check or putting their hands on you when you approached the table. Getting fresh, Ginny called it. When she had to wait on these guys, Mary Lee adopted a mousy camouflage, but if Jules couldn't cow them with her put-downs, she'd stall their orders or deliver the wrong food, dare them to call her on it. She could afford to hunger for a fight; the bartender was a big man. And anyway in the restaurant it was only locals who sometimes shouted red-faced or swung a clumsy punch and were relieved to be dissuaded from following through.

One night after Ginny had gone home and the band had already started playing, Jules turned her back on a table full of these guys and went to the bartender and said, Boot them, one of those jerks gave me the finger. Mary Lee was loading steins of draft beer onto a tray; she knew that if she'd come with the same complaint, the bartender would at least have gone over to the table. But Jules showed up for work with dilated eyes and had taken to sitting down with the band when they took a break and waving off customers who called for her. No, the bartender said. Mary Lee thought Jules would just refuse to wait on those men, but later she saw her delivering their drinks, smacking the glasses on the table.

When the band took a break, Jules sat down next to Colin and drank one of the beers she had delivered. Mary Lee refused Jules's offer of a sip from the bottle. The bartender had warned they'd be fired for drinking on the job. Colin leaned close to Jules, sweating from exertion, lifting his thin shirt from his skin so that Mary Lee could see the sharp rise of his collarbone, the swirl of hair at his nipples. Jules was watching him too, with the thoughtful expression of someone not sure whether to give in to impulse and buy some tempting, unnecessary trinket.

Colin announced that he and Jules had gotten tattoos yesterday. Jules had already shown hers to Mary Lee. A tiny rose where her belly sloped to her hipbone.

It really hurt, Jules said.

Show yours, Colin said. You show yours and I'll show mine.

Colin tugged at Jules, and she laughed. Slut! Shameless little hussy.

Ready to prove her right, Colin stood up and unbuckled his belt.

Bert and Joey hooted and stamped their feet, urging him on. Owen only glanced at Colin with an expression that seemed to say, Yes? What is it you wanted? Once Mary Lee had gone to the RV to borrow his iron—he'd told her she could—and she had found him lying on his bed reading, just like her. The shelved bunks around him held a knotted tangle of clothes and bedding, the almost alive disarray of his bandmates, as if they were still in that cramped space with him, but his sheets and blankets were taut and mitered, and he sat brutally straight, in a posture of coiled containment. He only slowly looked up to take in Mary Lee at the door and wait for her to ask him for something.

Still laughing, Jules batted at Colin's hands as if she could stop him. He carefully peeled back his jeans to expose the curve of his butt, a tattoo in Gothic script: Dharma Dogs.

Show yours, he said.

Jules looked at Owen. He may be cute, she said, but he's dumb as a rock.

Owen said, You just keep working at it. You'll catch up to him.

Jules held his gaze for a moment, and then she said she was going out for a cigarette. The bartender didn't glance up when she strolled past the bar with the beer bottle still clutched in her fist. Mary Lee had customers, and she forgot about Jules. But after a while Mary Lee began to be afraid she'd walked off the job.

She went outside. Usually Jules could be found on the bench beside the door, tapping ashes into a bucket of sand littered with butts. But she was not there. The parking lot was a patch of dirt raggedly carved out of the dark woods, and Mary Lee thought she saw someone moving in the trees. She walked out to check if Jules had wandered off to smoke with one of her cowboy pals. She cupped a hand to her mouth and called Jules's name.

The shapes back in the trees retreated. It wasn't funny for Jules to play games on her. But those pooled shapes took on the configuration of struggle. Mary Lee saw an arm swinging clumsily free. Julie! she shouted. Jules!

Jules came running at her from the darkness, stumbling into Mary Lee with such force that she turned her half around. Jules pushed her hard, and both of them ran back toward the lighted entrance of the building. Mary Lee's heart jolted when she heard the sound of running feet behind them, but then a car door slammed and an engine whined to life. When they reached the doorway, Jules sank to the bench. Her peach dress had been tugged open to her waist.

What happened? Mary Lee said.

Nothing, Jules said. Forget it.

You have to tell me.

Jules spoke with the halting slowness of surprise. These two guys came out behind me, chatting me up, and we're—God, I shouldn't have had that beer—somehow I'm walking with them through the parking lot. It didn't hit me what they were up to till they were dragging me back in the woods.

A welt was rising on her cheekbone just below her eye. Mary Lee began to tremble, but even then her habit of discipline held. I'm going inside to call the police.

Jules said, Look at my eyes. Do you think a cop might miss the fact that I'm stoned out of my mind?

Jules was still in shock. Mary Lee knew the line she should take: women often felt responsible for an attack.

She dug her nails into her palms. It's not your fault, she said.

I was stupid, that's all. Nothing happened.

Then Colin and Owen came out the door. Maybe Colin was looking for Jules so they could go smoke another joint, maybe they had come out, the way Colin sometimes did, to ask if Mary Lee and Jules actually worked here. But someone had come looking for them.

Colin sucked his breath between his teeth when he saw Jules. Jules didn't look up at him or tug at the dress, peeled back like flayed skin. Mary Lee leaned down to button it up for her, one, two, three, and then a button missing but her fingers couldn't stop searching for it.

Mary Lee said, Two guys dragged her out to the woods.

Jules pushed Mary Lee's hands away. I told you it was no big deal.

Where are they? Colin said. We'll take care of them.

They're long gone, Mary Lee said.

Colin got the same look on his face that the ranchers did when someone caught them by the arms before they could swing the next punch.

Get some ice, Owen said to Colin.

Owen had to give him a shove before he obeyed.

Colin came back with a bag of ice, but he was not the one to apply it. Owen took the ice from him and crouched to hold it to Jules's cheek. She put her hand over his, tilted her head back, and closed her eyes.

What entitled you to such tenderness? What had Mary Lee missed, refusing to fritter away her time? Some extravagance, with this return. No use crying over it.

Owen removed the ice and probed Jules's skin, and she flinched under that steady, cautious contact.

You'll have a shiner, he said.

Well, I walked away, Jules said. With nothing but a scratch.

She tried a smirk. I was so out of it. Strolling along with them, arm in arm.

Owen rose jerkily to his feet and stood over Jules, his fists clenched. What the fuck did you think would happen?

Mary Lee should have leapt to Jules's defense. But she felt the pull of what was in him. A hot rage. No, you couldn't walk away. You couldn't make any forays out there in the dark and come back a little astonished, still curious. The heat coming off Owen called up warmth in Mary Lee, this fellow feeling and not any other, not any game of seduction but a patient teaching of a more constant vigilance. She had to figure out how to survive, as he had figured out how to leave a decoy to be savaged in his place in the mess of that trailer or whatever else held him. Tonight Jules would sleep fine, but Mary Lee would lie awake in the box where they were kept.

Owen turned to Mary Lee and jabbed a finger at her. You! You stay smart!

She didn't say no. She didn't say, I don't want to.

The Dazzling World

Dismal, Cam was telling Judith. You show up for the casting call and sit on folding chairs in the hallway, and you look around and see that everyone's the same. All the guys look like you, because the director put out a call for middle-aged, bookish men. And all the actresses look alike too, the housewife type, all these slightly overweight women with stunned expressions.

Dismal might have described their present circumstances, sitting on a crowded bus that lurched at every hairpin turn of the road as it ascended through the dense mesh of tropical jungle. When the bus jerked over a rut, the people jammed in the aisle rocked and swayed in a motion that seemed as smooth as the parabolic arc of a whip but was felt in jolting increments, flesh and all its vulnerable softnesses smacked against other flesh, against the metal frames of the seats and the shifting contents of packages compressed between one body and another. The heat-fused blend of exhaust fumes and acrid human odors demanded resignation.

What if you didn't know what slot you were in? Judith said.

What if you showed up for a casting call thinking you were a coquette and had to take your seat with all the housewives?

Cam nodded. And nothing you can do about it. You can't disown the body that carts you around.

Cam had never complained to Judith before of this aspect of his journeyman trade as a stage actor, and she wondered, why now, when those casting-call hallways must have been air-conditioned. Did it come to mind because on this bus they were so distinct among all the dark-skinned, black-haired, stocky people?

She should have expected to feel supersized and overfed, encumbered with excess. When they arrived in Guatemala City, they had taken a taxi to the bus station, Judith reading the address to the taxi driver from the letter her sister had sent. She and Cam had hauled their luggage onto a local bus that would take them to the highland village near Dana's archaeological site. Pluming black smoke, the bus made arduous progress through the crowded streets of the city, and Judith counted one shop sign after another announcing *reparación*, every imaginable kind of salvage and repair, from cars to refrigerators and watches, asserting the essential condition of a poor country against any *turista* illusions. Before they had left the city limits, Cam said he didn't think he could take the heat even for the week they planned to spend with Dana.

The bus bounced over another rut, and the woman standing beside Cam lost her grip on her heavy bag, smacking it against his skull. Cam clapped a hand to his head, cursing; she'd been banging that bag against him the whole trip, and he'd refused Judith's offer to trade places. Cam reached for the bag, and the woman gripped it more tightly. An anxious flow of Spanish came from her mouth as they played tug-of-war. Cam smiled at the woman, gesturing his intent, the expansiveness of his physical language almost aggressive in their cramped circumstances, until finally he succeeded in getting her to relinquish the bag. Settling it in his lap, he said, Es más fácil.

After that, Cam and the woman were fast friends, though wariness never quite left her face as she tried to converse with him in the limited vocabulary they had in common. Making a fuss was Cam's way of encountering the world. It would be his loud voice that boomed out a protest when someone cut in line at the grocery store, prompting laughter, or his contentious remark about their neighbor's loud music late one night that would result in an invitation to the next party. It was something you got used to, his vague discontent. Judith had seen him through dozens of dark nights of the soul when he thought he should move to L.A. and really give this a shot or quit acting rather than subsist forever on scraps. She had weathered countless agonized discussions over whether they worked hard enough at their relationship or were truly compatible.

Last summer, after four years, they'd begun talking about marriage. They were in their late thirties; their friends had paired off with an air of finality. At least they might live together. A long search to find an apartment neither objected to, within reach on their small salaries. But the day Judith was supposed to drop off the security deposit, she had to meet a tight deadline for a biology text. Unable to scan into the computer her diagrams of cell processes and amino-acid structures, she raced to the publisher's office to deliver them in person. She forgot about the deposit and they lost the apartment, and Cam knew what this meant. When she could not tease him out of his conviction, she tried tit for tat: which one of them really wasn't sure? They were still living in separate apartments.

Judith was tired from their flight, and her eyes kept closing as she listened to Cam gamely fight on with the woman, struggling to be understood. When the bus slammed to a halt for the men in the road and one of them boarded the bus with his rifle slanted across his hip, she was roused from sleep to the strangest of strange worlds, unmoored, bewildered, submissive. She thought, this is what you hallucinate out of the most shameful reaches of your privilege, and she felt as if she had called down this threat on all the other passengers. The man with the rifle issued orders she had no hope of understanding. She reached reflexively for her purse, and Cam had to stop her. She followed him as he followed the lead of the other passengers, setting down packages and filing off the bus in silence.

Three men with rifles: one posted at the folding door of the bus and two who stood just beyond, lining up passengers by the side of the road. Cam held Judith's hand when they stepped off the bus, and she could not see the man who motioned them to join the others, could not lift her eyes from the coal surface of the rifle's barrel to his face. One of the armed men climbed back on the bus to go through their packages, and another began moving down the line of passengers, a hand out, palm up, to receive what little these people could cough up. Cam held Judith tight against him, and her clothing wicked up the sweat that soaked his shirt. Judith could only keep looking at the rifles. She had the strange need to be accurate in recording what she saw: barrel, scope, rifle stock. Cylinder, disk, cone.

She stared at the man's palm when it was finally thrust at her, mentally tracing the lines that crosshatched his skin, as if her eye were charting in advance the route her hand must follow with a pen. Cam clutched her tightly, but with his free hand he undid the clasp of her watch and surrendered it. One-handed, he managed to remove his own watch and tug his wallet from his back pocket.

They waited for the man to reach the end of the line. In the tense, expectant quiet, Cam could not help himself. He said in his loud voice, If these morons had any brains, they'd have waited for a tourist bus. The silence snapped in the air around them—crack of a whip, like the bodies jostling with the jerky motion of the bus—and Judith tugged at his sleeve and whispered, Shut up, shut up. She squeezed her eyes closed until whatever volley of sound might have followed on his booming voice did not come. For sure would not come.

Judith and Cam had taken a stab at marriage counseling, though they were not married. Fighting over the forgotten check in front of a third party led to Cam declaring that someone who did fussy little drawings for a living had to intend to be careless and Judith insisting they explore the semantics of *fussy, little*. Was this a stalemate? Judith thought she could be patient. She had always taken pleasure in the methodical habits of her work, starting her day by putting on a Bach CD and finishing a second cup of coffee while she lined up her pens and taped tracing paper over the layout grid on which she did her rough sketch. But now she could work only in silence. Some new restlessness forced her to get up from the drafting table to clean the kitchen or run errands. She would set out for the corner store and end up walking for blocks. Judith had always been disinclined to venture beyond air-conditioning and indoor plumbing, not nearly so hardy as her sister, professionally immune to heat, bugs, dust, happily seducing her archaeology students in Texas to accompany her every summer. When Judith decided to accept Dana's invitation to visit during the field season, Cam had not been meant to accompany her. He signed on later, after they had agreed to quit therapy. She had disciplined herself not to anticipate too closely what the trip might be like. She could never have imagined the men with rifles.

It was natural to want to keep talking about it once she and Cam arrived at Dana's house, and natural to go on as planned and not to balk at the ordinary even if Judith could still feel her pulse skip and Cam started at every noise. They admired the embroidered *huipils,* stiff T-shaped blouses that Dana had tacked up like posters on the walls of the one-room house—a shack on a slab of concrete, really—and were interested when Dana pointed out the stylized image of a bat in the intricate needlework, link between the living and the ancient Mayan past. In the roofed porch at the back of the house, they helped Dana make dinner on a camp stove, and later they drank tepid lager, sitting cross-legged on the futon that would be Cam and Judith's bed. When Cam said Dana might have warned them, Dana snapped that they were more likely to be robbed at home. The robbers had carried rifles because handguns were nearly impossible to come by here.

Well, that makes me feel better, Cam said.

Dana punched him in the arm. Whenever the three of them got together, a lot of slugging and *hey asshole* went on between her and Cam, the chest thumping of two high school boys.

By any measure, Judith and Cam had been lucky. The robbers had taken off with their loot on motorcycles. When the passengers funneled back onto the bus, whole and unharmed, they repatriated the torn-open packages strewn on the seats and wiped up squashed melons from the floor in a tamped, cooperative silence. The robbers had not bothered to take Judith's and Cam's passports, and they had not found the traveler's checks Cam had rolled inside a pair of socks. When they were resettled in their seats, Cam cupped Judith's face in his hands and kissed her.

Judith peeled the label from her bottle of lager—why did a Guatemalan beer have a German name?—and asked Dana if they would visit the site tomorrow.

Don't expect a royal tomb or anything, Dana said. These are ordinary dwellings. We're fishing out the bones they threw away after meals, shards of pottery, earrings, seeds. These people were not wasteful. In this one little house we excavated, they'd mounted the handles of broken jars right into the walls so they could hang things up, keep the place neat. We've been doing some infrared prospecting, and—

Geek, Cam said.

Dana laughed. I won't deny it. Mayanist conferences are worse than Trekkie conventions.

I wish you had something besides beer, Cam said. Situations involving firearms require a good stiff drink. Blunt reality is so blinding.

Right, Dana said testily. Americans go around the world so well padded.

I didn't mean it that way, Cam said. Whoever you are, you go along in a fog of going along. I've never even seen a rifle before. But for as long as it's pointed at you, you're stripped of all stupidity. You know your life's a contingency.

Cam reached over to Judith and gripped her hand.

Judith said, Is that why you had to see if those guys could take a little teasing?

Cameron, Dana said. I think Judith's heard enough on the subject.

Dana and Cam exchanged a look of complicity. Sometimes this made Judith feel as if she'd been granted some lifelong dispensation she hadn't really earned. She and Dana had shared an uneventful, contented childhood; even Judith's memories were tinted pastel blue and peach, like some doctor's waiting room designed to impart tranquillity to the patients. Only one thing out of the ordinary had ever happened to Judith. She was twenty when she hooked up with her sad-eyed, gentle boy and couldn't have known what Hollander would do. He had grown up in a trailer with a mother who lived on disability, and he told Judith how, first thing in the morning, his mother dropped to her knees before the coffee table and ran a finger over its surface to collect grains of cocaine and rub them over her gums. His was a story Judith could not recognize, but he could in telling it persuade her that his survival had not hardened him. Persuade her, as no one else had ever bothered to do, that she was essential to him, could counter his confession that he didn't want to live, stay his hand. Until the night they were driving home in his rattletrap Toyota and he swerved across the median strip into oncoming traffic, having promised her for miles that he would do it, prompting intent negotiations that had the searing certainty of love. She walked away with a few broken bones; he died of his injuries.

Cam settled an arm over Judith's shoulder, protectiveness articulated even in the fan of his fingers—the good thing and the bad thing about being with an actor—and filed another grievance: Couldn't Dana have managed to own a fan?

You get used to the heat, Dana said, scrambling to her feet. I've got to get up at the crack of dawn.

Taking her toothbrush from the shelf by the back door, she reminded them to watch for scorpions in the outhouse.

After Dana went out to the washbasin on the back porch, Cam said, Me and my big mouth.

In a moment he would engulf her in his arms.

It's no big deal, Judith said.

I'm sorry for all the rest of it too, Cam said, his voice thready with emotion. What I've put you through.

Judith said nothing. She had grown wary of accepting apologies from him. They had wasted their last session with the marriage counselor. Cam had complained Judith never waited up for him when he came over after a performance, and she said he had his own key, and he said the duplicate she'd given him got stuck in the lock, and she yanked her key ring from her pocket and offered to trade him on the spot. Cam came home with her after that session instead of going back to his own apartment, and when they arrived at her door, that symbolic door, they dissolved into laughter. This made it easy to fall into bed together. Except that when they made love, he cried.

Now he kissed her hungrily. In the hot night the heat his body transmitted was oppressive, his skin slick on hers, even his tongue a hot probe.

Dana would come back in a few minutes, and then they would wash up, and all three of them would sleep in the same room. Judith would not have to answer Cam's ardor.

◆   ◆   ◆   ◆   ◆

The tour Dana gave them did not proceed in any orderly fashion, even if the tell itself was carefully marked off in six-by-six-meter squares, hundreds of them, bounded by taut rope barriers. With Guillermo, her counterpart from a Guatemalan university, Dana had spent two years just mapping the site; they might hope to dig maybe twenty squares a season. Only a few had been excavated so far. When they dug the trenches, the workers left the soil intact at the north and east border of each square, a strip Dana called the balk, preserved undisturbed as a chronological reference point. With a spiral notebook stuffed in the pocket of her cargo pants, Dana scrambled in and out of trenches to confer with the Guatemalan workmen or jumped over a row of baskets filled with soil or whirled to point out to Cam and Judith the flash of a scarlet macaw in the trees that flanked the cleared site. The workmen kept calling Dana by some nickname, which she translated only when pressed. La Cabrita, Little Goat.

Dana took Cam and Judith to watch two of her students work at a sifter, a rectangular fine-mesh screen set on waist-high supports. One of the students sifted soil onto the screen while the other nimbly fished out loose stones that could damage fragile artifacts. The soil sent up puffs of dust as it drifted to the ground.

Until about thirty years ago, Dana said, anthropologists made all kinds of wrong assumptions about the Maya, because they hadn't decoded their language and no one had bothered to excavate ordinary dwellings.

Dana turned abruptly to shout at a workman hauling a

basket out of the trench, and he grinned and replied in words that lacked the musicality of Spanish.

Most of the local workmen speak Quiche, Dana said. Language of their ancestors. Another thing anthropologists didn't bother to investigate until recently. There's a site in Mexico where they started using screens with very fine mesh, and they recovered all these tiny bones from burial sites. No thicker than a needle. Turned out to be the bones of these little toads whose flesh has hallucinogenic properties. If you were somebody important, it was your duty to have visions. Drugs were not enough to do the job. These folks were into ritual bloodletting. Kinky stuff like shredding your tongue on a rope studded with thorns.

What have you found here? Cam said. Anything to get your name up in lights?

Dana gave him a severe look. This is work that takes patience. We have to label everything and record it on the computer. Then we've got to figure out how to manipulate the database so it pops out something useful.

They wandered around the site, getting in the way of people who had work to do, and Dana divided her attention between enlightening the ignorant and taking care of business. When Guillermo wanted her help with something, she decided Cam and Judith might like to try their hand at trench work. It would be a treat.

Cam was eager at first; he'd been eager for everything since they'd gotten back on the bus yesterday. But Dana forgot them, too absorbed in her work to remember they'd been deposited in the trench without water to drink, without hats or the bandannas that the workers tied bandit-style over their noses to filter dust. You broke the soil with a pick, just enough to loosen it, and then used a trowel or your bare hands to scrape away dirt, working with a brush if you hit anything larger than a pebble, quickly discovering the futility of the task. The only break in the monotony was the occasional outburst from the howler monkeys far off in the forest, mournful preternatural cries that made Cam jump every time they erupted.

A boy came by with a bucket of water. The other workers took turns dipping a ladle in the bucket, but Judith and Cam couldn't risk drinking anything that wasn't bottled. Judith took the opportunity to stretch. Her back had not healed as completely as her broken bones. She awoke every morning with a dull back-ache—would know she was awake because of it—which faded once she got up and bothered her now only because she had been crouching for so long.

Cam complained that Dana had a weird idea of fun.

Judith didn't really mind; she knew tedium might open onto something else. She had to make painstaking calculations to scale her drawings, working within rigid specifications. But the tactile pleasure of seaming ink onto smooth paper or dipping a wet brush into the paste of gouache was its own reward, and if you were deep enough into the task, sometimes you were startled by the beauty it would yield, the spirals of chromosomes in an onion root cell, the radial symmetry of chromosomes aligned along the mitotic spindle during cell division, the exquisite snowflake intricacy of colonial algae viewed under a microscope.

When the boy came by with water again, Cam drank from the ladle with the other men. Judith didn't warn him about parasites or contaminated water. Sooner or later, Cam would be lured by prohibitions. Once, on a trip to Maui, he'd deserted her at the beach, taking off with a teenage boy who'd promised him marijuana. She had waited an hour for him to return. The boy might have robbed him; Cam could have been arrested; he came back knowing the boy's name, which hotel he worked at as a bellboy, exactly where the houses of service workers were hidden from view.

And this time too there were unforeseen gains. With artful exaggeration, Cam mimed his way through negotiations for bandannas so the two of them could cover their mouths against the dust.

When he dropped into the trench and handed her a bandanna, Judith said, We can just quit. It's not a long walk back to Dana's house.

She promised she'd fetch us to go to the waterfall this afternoon, Cam said. She probably snuck off with old Guillermo.

On their tour Dana had introduced them to Guillermo with an offhandedness that Judith and Cam had quickly deciphered.

We could go without her, Cam said.

The waterfall was not far, but Dana had warned that the jungle quickly reclaimed the path, and you had to take a heavy stick to beat the bushes for snakes.

Maybe she'll have time to take us tomorrow, Judith said.

We only have a week. You always let other people dictate the agenda.

Don't you remember any of the lessons of therapy? Judith said. Don't globalize. Stick to the specific when you gripe.

That whole thing was a mistake, he said.

Was it his agitation or hers that evoked the plaintive chords of restlessness? Judith pressed her hand flat against the cool dirt wall of the trench.

I got a job offer for fall, Cam said. Teaching drama to high school kids. It's a good school. It's only part-time, so I could still swing rehearsals if I had to.

That would be nice, she said. To teach.

I'd get health insurance. I'd be able to pay the rent. He sighed. I'm at the point where maybe I should resign myself.

His head jerked at another distant ululation from the howler monkeys. God damn it! he said. I'm still so shook up. Aren't you?

He closed his trembling hand over hers. *Why* aren't you? he said.

A trick question. He would have in mind some reason other than the one she would give. He had always treated her unbidden and shuddering memories of Hollander with a tactful awe, coaxed her to confess something more, something else. Not satisfied with her vindictive answer—*the hateful little shit taught me a lesson*—he would gently persist in trying to find in her some tragic, transfiguring mark. Bent on flushing an answer that would stun them both. She used to relish being the audience for the surprises Cam staged every year on the anniversary of their meeting. Once he wangled someone's sailboat and took her out on the bay. Another time he presented her with a forties dress and a garter and nylons filched from stage props and took her to a swing-dancing lesson. Had she disappointed him each time, failed to rise to the occasion?

They had been hiking for an hour, ascending into the deep green of the mountain range. Cam and Dana had started out bickering in a careless way that made it sport—why couldn't Dana make time for them until their third day here, and how could Cam possibly grasp the first thing about the responsibilities of a steady job?—but had given themselves up, like Judith, to the dazzling world they had entered. The caution they had to exercise—beating bushes for snakes, plucking bugs from one another's shirts, gently bending back overhanging branches so they would not do unnecessary damage—did not seem to impede their progress. A butterfly stained a cobalt blue settled on Dana's outstretched hand. Orange mushrooms clustered on a fallen log, a row of bright buttons. A flock of tiny finches rose into the sky like a swirl of brightly colored confetti. A band of howler monkeys, throats vibrating with their eerie cries, fled in the branches of the trees and then stopped to squint at them and hurl insults.

Dana had complained that with Cam along, she wouldn't get time to herself with Judith, but most of Judith's time had been spent alone with Cam, waiting in that little house for Dana to show up at the promised hour. Cam wouldn't quit bothering Judith. So many revelations had struck him in their short time here, and she had to remind him they'd declared a moratorium on talking about their relationship. Yesterday she had found a deck of cards and talked him into playing poker, just to keep him occupied. They had only a handful of coins between them, and when Judith ran out of money, they made dares instead of bets. Could Judith touch the hairy centipede crawling up the wall? Could Cam finish off a bottle of beer without pausing once for breath? Could Judith remove her bra without removing her shirt? In the midday heat it felt good to forfeit an article of clothing, and another and another. Maybe because they knew Dana might come back at any moment and they had to be quick, Cam did not hold Judith's face in his hands and declare how much he loved her, and Judith did not have to stop his hand from lingering long enough to locate hurt.

They could hear the roar of the waterfall long before they could see it, but even their anticipation did not lessen its breathtaking effect when they broke out of the woods onto the bank of the river. The water fell several hundred feet down a craggy rock face, a cumulus cloud of froth at its base.

For a long time they stood still and breathed air that had been churned to a cool mist. Then Cam wanted to clamber up the steep, cantilevered slope. He thought it might be possible to squeeze in between the face of the rock and the falling water.

What for? Dana said.

There's a peak moment here, Cam said. If you're willing to take your opportunity.

Dana said she was afraid of heights.

Come on, Cam said to Judith. That won't bother you.

In his wake, she thought she could manage it. He was tall enough that he could remain upright as he found his footing, and wherever she got stuck, he pulled her up to the next outcrop of rock. Scrambling after him, she felt a twinge in her lower back, a brief sharp ache that had long ago become familiar, reassuring.

Halfway up, they stopped. Judith was sweating from her effort despite the water-churned air. She looked down at the water swirling in the pool below, at Dana shading her eyes with her hand.

Judith said, I'm dizzy.

No you're not, Cam said.

He inched horizontally across a narrow ledge of rock until he could peer into the darkness behind the sheet of falling water. To be heard over its rushing noise, he had to shout.

There's room to squeeze in, he crowed.

Down below Dana was waving him off.

Cam waved back at her and pinwheeled his arms as if he were about to lose his balance.

Don't tease her, Judith said.

Cam pressed his back to the rock face and edged beneath the curtain of water.

Judith could see moss furring the wet rock. It looks slippery, she said.

He said, I dare you, but the carelessness was gone from his voice.

He put an arm out for her. Come on. Come with me.

Judith shook her head.

Cam inched farther beneath the curtain of water until he was only dimly visible. From out of that darkness came his booming voice. Oh God! God! God!

Judith did not wait for him but started down the rock face by herself. She didn't have to look back to know that he'd made it out without falling, because Dana was enacting relief below, smacking her forehead and shaking her fist.

Dana would have let it go, but Cam could not.

When he reached them, he nailed Judith. Why'd you hold back?

I must be afraid of heights after all, Judith said.

You don't trust me, do you? Cam said. At bottom you don't trust me.

Cam reached for Judith, caught her arm. This is the story of our relationship, he said. I can't get you to take that one little step closer.

Dana whirled around and thumped her fist on his chest. Shut up. Shut up, or walk back alone.

She returned to the path, her walking stick held like a lance. Judith shook off Cam and followed her. She willed herself not to listen for him behind them. She willed herself not to turn around and deliver all the grudges that jostled within her for pride of place. They hadn't lasted a day on this trip before he broke their agreement on talking about the relationship. They had not made love for weeks when they had their stupid debate over the key, but that ridiculous transaction had been enough to rekindle his desire. Unable to keep his mouth shut like everyone else, he'd risked provoking those men who had boarded the bus, as if he'd wanted their attention, their rifles, aimed at him—at *her*, gripping his sleeve. He'd forced her to dig at her memories until she yielded proof she was tainted: yes, she still dreamed about thumping over the median strip, anticipating impact, and yes, Hollander had made sure, had unclipped his seat belt so that he'd fly into the windshield and shatter every bone in his face.

Walking single file on the narrow path, Judith could see only the working of Dana's shoulder muscles, vigorously applying that stick to the bushes, as she talked.

Don't let the bastard torture you, Dana said.

I thought you liked him, Judith said.

That's a separate issue.

Judith's grudges were compacted in a tight space, all bunched together. She had forgotten the check for the security deposit. She just forgot.

◆ ◆ ◆ ◆ ◆

Cam took off for two days on his own. To give you time alone with your sister, he said. Judith wasn't surprised; over the past year they had ended up arguing most times they saw each other, because they could tolerate each other's presence only so long before one of them was reminded of their failure. They would have to retreat for a week or two before trying again.

Judith did not mind being taken along to the site when Dana could not tear herself away from work. Judith liked being drenched in information she was not obliged to retain, walking along beside Dana as she read the balk, studying its stratified layers for clues to how soil had been deposited at the site. She liked helping Dana sort shards of pottery, rearranging them on a table in the ceramics shed, trying to reconstitute a whole that could be glued back together. Jigsaw puzzles had obsessed them when they were kids, little girls in love with finite assignments. Both of them had an eye for visual pattern, could scan the whole and intuit what fit in a gap, though Dana was more stubborn, less likely to retreat from a wrong guess. In their murmured conversations about the shards, Dana would toss off something about Judith's relationship. Dana's clarity tended to take the form of commands: Take a page from Guillermo and me. Who needs the hassle? Tell Cam to put up or shut up. Beat him to the punch, at least get that satisfaction. If you don't have the strength to boot him out, stay here with me. We can always use an artist.

On the morning Cam came back, Judith was working at the mesh screen with one of Dana's students. She had just found a tiny bead lodged in the mesh, dirt encrusted but a mottled green that made her wish it might be jade. She held it in her palm to show it to the archaeology student, who was assertively dashing her hopes when Cam joined them.

Judith dropped the bead into the student's hand before she gave Cam a quick, assessing glance. Don't expect me to ask if you had fun.

I debated whether I should just show up when they boarded the plane.

She had prepared for the possibility that she might not see him until she caught her flight home.

She said, I was thinking about not showing up at all.

I meant to do you a favor by removing my miserable self.

He thrust his hand out to show her what lay cupped in his palm. Two small clay flutes, shaped for use, complete with finger holes and mouthpieces that had been cleverly molded in the pleasing curves of animal snouts.

Peace offering, he said. One for you, one for Dana. Take your pick.

The warm terra-cotta color of the flutes drew the eye, compelled her hand to close over one of them.

Cam said, Did I spoil everything?

With a part of himself, he would have liked Judith to say yes.

No talk about us, she said.

She turned back to her work. He did not speak to her again, but he stood close enough that his shadow fell across the screen.

This hovering, this longing to settle all accounts. She'd lied to him twice about her boy. When Cam would not be satisfied with her admission that Hollander was a hateful little shit, she had lied to him again. She knew Hollander had smashed his face only because someone had told her. Cam would have pressed her: Was it that she couldn't bear to look in Hollander's direction or that she refused? Wanting her to declare, one way or the other.

After the car slammed to a halt, she stared at the cracked windshield. She couldn't feel any pain. Didn't yet know her luck. Just the ache of this dissipation beginning in her. She let her eye traverse the flourishing boundary lines still fracturing the glass, still dividing the one thing into many, so many she'd never count them all.

Judith waited for the heat or thirst or her silence to dislodge Cam. She waited until Dana came by to check in.

Hey, asshole, Dana said, and she swatted Cam with the notebook rolled in her hand, old pal, old buddy. He offered the flute, which she accepted with alacrity and promptly shoved into the deep pocket of her cargo pants.

You can come with me if you're not squeamish, Dana said to Cam. The guys think they found a skeleton. Our first one.

She turned to Judith. You don't have to come.

Of course Judith would come. Judith always wanted to see.

When they got to the trench, Dana dropped her notebook at its edge and jumped down, but so many workers had clustered around the face of the soil wall that Judith and Cam stayed where they were. She crouched beside him, clutching the smooth cylinder of the flute he had given her.

The workers had exposed in the dirt a solid, hard surface, nothing very startling. But Dana's expert hands loosened the soil, and every so often she called for a brush to sweep at the surface of the trench wall before she went back to digging with her fingers. Patiently she worked until she uncovered the globe of a small skull, pressed against the ball-and-socket joint of a shoulder.

Un pequeño, said one of the workers standing beside her.

Dana took a breath and stepped back. A child, she called up to Cam and Judith.

The silence that had up until now been tense with anticipation took on another quality entirely. In this expectancy Judith felt the other, the suspended uncertainty about what might follow on the sound of Cam's booming voice.

For this child, whom they could never name, who must have been ordinary, a child the same as any other, the silence held. The bones preserved for so long had the darkened patina of wood burnished by the touch of many hands. Twelve hundred years in the ground had stripped from this body the taint of fear and sorrow but somehow left an irreducible beauty. No chemical process could account for this, any more than it could account for the algae cells that Judith drew, each one exquisite and distinct in its crystalline symmetry.

The breeze suddenly picked up, stirring the loose soil at the lip of the trench, raising a visible veil of dust.

A man in the trench below said something softly, his open arms held up to the sky. And Cam, reading the gesture against the warp and weft of his own eagerness, called out, It's the spirit flying.

Judith still held the flute in her hand, her fingertips having found the perfect depressions made for them.

Slender Little Thing

A boy knocked her up at nineteen and left her and that was that. Don't think of it as a door slammed shut because Cerise found work, the only kind for which she was qualified but a good kind—raising someone else's children, all that was demanded of her a cooing love and light housekeeping. Nine hours a day Cerise lived like a swank, and her little girl went to day care and sometimes to relatives if Cerise had to stay late or spend a weekend with the Griffins' two boys. She loved those boys, and Mason and Connor loved her; she had some hand in their shining futures. With the boys Cerise had to do things their mother's way, striving to hover near that mark, as if she was never really alone with them, and this was what she could save back—hoard—for Sophie, that delicious feeling of going home on the bus to *just us two*. After both boys started high school, the Griffins helped Cerise get a place at the nursing home, as what they called a personal care technician, which didn't require taking courses or administering the correct doses of medication. She could learn how to make a bed with someone in it. She could croon an angry old man into holding still for a sponge bath, intimacy to which both of them must submit. Cerise had practice at the patience she needed once Sophie turned sixteen: her marvel of a girl woke up one day to rail as if all along she'd been waiting for the chance to lodge a complaint, and when Cerise came home from work she'd better hear it and not flinch. Girls went through a phase of hating their mothers. Sophie was so smart, Cerise didn't have to worry when she found the marijuana tucked inside a sock in her daughter's top drawer, when her daughter brought home a scruffy man of twenty who might pocket her virginity but could never outwit Sophie's careful plans for college, when her daughter tried to badger her into screaming back. One day Cerise and Sophie would be friends again, and don't think of it.

Don't think of it as a door slammed shut because Cerise found work, the only kind for which she was qualified but a good kind—raising someone else's children, all that was demanded of her a cooing love and light housekeeping. After Dale took off on her, she had tried to get her GED. Tuesday nights she took adult ed in a high school classroom that smelled of sweat. By the end of every class the pages of her workbook were flecked with oily bits of pencil eraser. It did not help to try hard. Her eyes could not align numbers in columns or prevent letters from coagulating; these things evaded her even if she pounced on them. She must have inherited the problem from her mother, who had managed to give Cerise a name she shared with no else.

Working as a nanny came easy to Cerise, though Mr. and Mrs. Griffin were both doctors and could not always come home when they said they would. Mason was two years older than

Sophie, Connor a year younger. Cerise had a sweet-smelling new baby to hold, and Mason was such a talker and planner, making forts from sofa cushions or building a tower of wood blocks and telling her all the time what he was thinking. Four years old, and his skull was stuffed with facts. If she couldn't read to Mason, he had books on tape, and she'd hold him in her lap and turn the page every time a little bell rang on the tape. When he was at kindergarten and the baby was napping, she could sneak a cigarette on the deck and then watch TV, because if she didn't get to all the housekeeping, Mrs. Griffin would say, the children come first. Mrs. Griffin took great care over everything that had to do with the two boys. Connor must not be left to cry; if Mason misbehaved, Cerise could give him a timeout for two minutes and no more; when she fed the boys, she should consult a list of nutritious foods taped to the refrigerator door. Cerise felt shored up by all that transmitted knowledge. And once in a while a little cornered. It didn't hurt Sophie to have ice cream or a candy bar, and if Cerise took the boys with her on errands, she could not always say no when Mason pleaded for a treat.

Cerise could mark the passage of time—the years of Sophie and the boys growing up—by the shift in her morning bus schedule. When Mason started first grade, she had to arrive earlier to get him ready for school—she had the use of the Griffins' car by then—and Mrs. Griffin did not mind if she brought Sophie with her and dropped her off after she delivered Mason. Sophie got to sit in front beside her; Mrs. Griffin did not allow her children in the front seat. Once Sophie started grade school, Cerise could take her by bus before she arrived at the Griffins'. A few years later Sophie could take the bus alone, and Cerise left her at the bus stop. Before they went their separate ways in the morning, she and Sophie locked their pinkie fingers together and tugged five times, chanting L-O-V-E-U before letting go. They were still doing this when Sophie started middle school and could leave the apartment after Cerise, her keychain clipped to her backpack. Cerise would wake Sophie before she left for work, and Sophie would groggily snake a hand out from under the covers, her pinkie finger already hooked.

When Sophie got into Lowell, the academic high school, she had to get up earlier to take two buses across town. Only after Cerise got the job at the nursing home did they again leave the house at the same time. Like meeting a stranger to be in the house with Sophie when she got ready: ironing her hair with a curling iron, plucking eyebrows attenuated to perfect commas, unearthing a cache of jars and tubes to make up her face. Maybe Sophie had started to be fussy in middle school, and Cerise just hadn't been there to witness it. Sophie would stand before the mirror wailing that she had nothing to wear and demand that Cerise produce something, when she had been doing her own laundry since she was eleven. Cerise made the mistake once of checking the dryer for clean clothes. Already late for work, she threw the clothes into the laundry basket to dump at her daughter's feet. Sophie had a fit. Dirty clothes went into the laundry basket, not clean ones, and Cerise knew it, she knew Sophie couldn't wear anything contaminated with all those germs and bodily fluids, but she just didn't care.

Cerise went out to her bus stop in a huff, and Sophie dashed off to hers, sure she'd get a tardy on her report card, and all because of her mother. Cerise's bus came first, and as it passed the corner where Sophie waited, she glimpsed her daughter, a slender little thing in an oversized sweatshirt and tight jeans.

Cerise could catalog in intimate detail the contents of her daughter's heavy backpack: textbooks neatly covered with brown paper, spiral notebooks labeled by subject, pens and a calculator secured in separate compartments, all of it organized as if to invite an inspection. Cerise pressed her palm to the glass. They'd never fussed over good-byes, and Sophie had no reason to look up.

Nine hours a day Cerise lived like a swank, and her little girl went to day care and sometimes to relatives if Cerise had to stay late or spend a weekend with the Griffins' two boys. The boys had done so well. Mason was at Harvard, studying to be an architect, and Connor was musical. Cerise was still invited to his piano recitals. Sophie was a bright kid too, a math whiz. Her father must have been smarter than Cerise thought. Sophie saw numbers in color: the number one was a pale blue, two a sunny yellow, three a Kelly green. If she looked at a license plate, the numbers left a tracery of color in her mind. If she studied an algebraic equation, a shimmer of color hinted at the answer. The boys grew up sloppy—Cerise was forever picking up after them, and their rooms became so chaotic that Mrs. Griffin told her, Just pick up a few things when you dust and don't torment yourself—but Sophie was neat. Her clothes were hung in the closet; she never forgot her house key; she would rewrite a homework assignment if a page got torn or wrinkled. She did not ask why her father had left, only where he was, as if he were one more thing she must keep in its place. Cerise could not tell her where he had gone.

Cerise was home now when Sophie returned from school— her shift at the nursing home ended at four—and if Sophie wasn't working that afternoon she came straight home to shower, to scour herself after riding the bus, holding on to a rail that hundreds of hands touched each day. When Cerise was making dinner, Sophie demanded to know if she had washed her hands before touching the food. She read the ingredients on every package, refused to eat meat, demanded to know if gum contained any animal by-products. The window in her bedroom had settled badly in its frame, and she stuffed rags at its perimeter so spiders would not get into the room through the cracks. When she went to bed, she rolled a towel at the base of the door, so spiders could not come in that way while she slept. If she found a spider, she would call for Cerise to come and squash it.

Cerise always answered this summons. It was the way Sophie called for her. Cerise knew from work which needs could be pared away from a person and which must be met. You could always recognize it in someone's voice, even if they could speak only gibberish. Of all the things sick old people could let go of—had to—shame was among the last, but even if that went, some need, some last small thing, took its place. One of her patients, Mrs. Andrews, who smelled faintly of urine even after her bath, would meekly raise her hips for her diapers to be changed but cry if Cerise could not find her tube of lipstick. For another, Mr. Petersen, Cerise was careful to tuck a towel around his waist and avert her face when she soaped the creases of his groin. She had seen her coworkers slap an ambulatory patient down on a stool in the communal shower and efficiently strip off clothes as if they were plucking feathers from dead chickens. Cerise was never hasty.

Sophie was not closing her fist over some last small thing,

not relinquishing but multiplying her needs. No longer was she satisfied for Cerise simply to crush a spider's body with a balled-up tissue. Sophie was sure that it had been a female spider, its body full of microscopic eggs, and Cerise must wash the wall with disinfectant, or hundreds of baby spiders would hatch and come after Sophie. How could Sophie allow that man to touch her? Cerise knew from experience what a man his age wanted from a sixteen-year-old girl. A stock boy at the drugstore where Sophie worked after school, a high-school dropout, and the one time Cerise had met him, too lazy to fit his belt through all the belt loops on his baggy jeans. Sophie, who sat up late at night finishing papers and already kept a file for college applications, did not even bother to defend him to Cerise.

Cerise loved those boys, and Mason and Connor loved her; she had some hand in their shining futures. When Mason came home from his second year at college in December, he came to the apartment to deliver a Christmas gift. Mrs. Griffin always sent a basket of perfect fruit and tiny jam jars and remembered how much Cerise loved chocolate and tucked a gift certificate into the card. Mason stood at the door, taking in the living room: the sofa bed where Cerise slept and her dresser and an armchair and a coffee table that had once belonged to his family and a Persian carpet, faded but real, that Cerise had asked for when Mrs. Griffin redid her family room. As long as the huge basket was in his arms, Mason was awkward, ashamed to recognize these possessions in their new surroundings. Even his wood blocks had fitted together precisely, unpainted, unvarnished chunks of maple sanded so smooth a hand would glide over their surfaces. He looked at Cerise as if *she* were misplaced in this crowded room.

After Cerise took the basket from Mason, they sat in the kitchen having coffee. He told her how cold it was in Boston in winter and admitted, when she pressed him, that he didn't do well in all his classes. He shrugged. If they don't interest me, I don't bother much. Hard to imagine something that didn't interest him. In the span of half an hour he informed her that the development of dwarf wheat had saved one billion people in India from starvation, that in Idaho it was illegal to give another person more than fifty pounds of chocolate as a gift, that Alzheimer's disease was caused by plaque forming in the brain. He asked how she liked nursing. She had spent more than a decade happily at his beck and call; he would understand.

They want you to get so many patients processed in an hour, she said, and it's no point just getting through your day. It's if this one feels better with a little lipstick on and you can sit to look at a picture they want to show you, just for a minute.

When Sophie got home from her shift at the drugstore—three more afternoons a week when she could be with Jackson—she did not sit with them but stood in the kitchen doorway in the blue vest she was required to wear at work, giving sullen answers to Mason's questions about where she was thinking of going to school and tugging at the name tag on her vest.

You'd like Harvard, he said.

To get into Harvard, Sophie said, you have to spend your summer doing volunteer work in France or building clinics in Costa Rica.

Mason gave Cerise another look of apology. He said, I went to Belgium.

Sophie smirked and left to take a shower. She knew everything already, Sophie did.

Mason was gone by the time Sophie came back to the kitchen, her long hair a wet cord trailing over her shoulder, to poke at the gift basket. Cerise was sitting by the window having a cigarette, swatting smoke so it wouldn't blow into the room. That's Swiss chocolate, Cerise said. Sophie read the ingredients on the package, her face keen with suspicion, and then tore open the package to inspect the chocolate. See that? she said. It's gone white. That means it's been exposed to heat. It's no good anymore. You have to throw it out.

With the boys Cerise had to do things their mother's way, striving to hover near that mark, as if she was never really alone with them, and this was what she could save back—hoard—for Sophie, that delicious feeling of going home on the bus to *just us two*. Sometimes when she was kept late at the Griffins' and had to serve the boys a quick dinner, Cerise would pick Sophie up from a friend's house at seven or so, and she would be too tired to make another meal, and even if Sophie had school the next day, they'd stop at Blockbuster on the way home to pick up a video, popcorn, and those spicy red candies, Hot Tamales. Getting back on the bus with Sophie's hand closed in hers, Cerise would crave the moment when they'd enter the apartment. They'd make the popcorn and pull out the sofa bed and arrange pillows at their backs and curl up together to watch some girl movie and sink into the happiness of no more to do for the day, laughing at the movie or hiding from each other their sniffles at the sad parts. To get up from that bed, a boat in an ocean, seemed hardly possible, and though they didn't talk much, their exchanges were intensely solicitous: Oh, you stay put, I'll make the popcorn. No, you let me get up this time. I'll get the ashtray for you, Mama.

After the boys started high school, the Griffins helped Cerise get a place at the nursing home, as what they called a personal care technician, which didn't require taking courses or administering the correct doses of medication. No need to sweat over words and numbers that clumped into knots or to worry over giving an injection. If an air bubble got in the syringe, you could kill someone. Cerise would rather fold clean sheets into oblong packets or gently swab the spiraled folds of someone's ear. When she thanked Mrs. Griffin for helping her find the job, Mrs. Griffin said she was the one who had to be grateful, for all Cerise had given her boys. Cerise could not pronounce the names of the practice pieces Connor got from his piano teacher—all the extra vowels of French, the grumbling consonants of German—but she'd delivered him for his lessons and had been the first to see the teacher was not right for Connor. In silence the woman sat beside him on the piano bench, rapping his wrists to keep them level and digging her knuckle between his shoulder blades when he didn't sit up straight. Cerise spoke to his parents: I don't think you want that for him. Mrs. Griffin took her at her word and found a better teacher. What Cerise knew, she knew, and Mrs. Griffin took it as a gift.

It was like giving Sophie a gift to hand her the checkbook and the bills at the end of every month. She was such a whiz! She did all the calculations in her head and staggered the bills so Cerise would never bounce a check. At ten Sophie had relished this evidence of her competence. Even now, when she rushed through the chore, she never made mistakes; she stacked the bills with the invoice sticking out of each envelope before she began writing the checks. While they sat at the table, Sophie handing over the checks for a signature, Cerise asked if there was enough in the bank account to cover the extra checks Sophie would write in January for her college application fees. Sophie said she would narrow her list to five.

Is five enough? Cerise said.

You could stop smoking for a month, Sophie teased, and then I could do six.

Oh, I should, Cerise said. And I could put off getting new shoes. That's another sixty dollars.

If Cerise bought a cheaper pair of orthopedic shoes for work, they wore out so fast, she saved nothing by it. And cheap shoes made her bunions hurt.

Oh, get the damn shoes! Sophie said.

Cerise apologized. I just want to see you set up right. No mistakes.

Sophie proved that she knew what Cerise was getting at by putting her hands over her ears, her response whenever Cerise tried to talk to her about sex. Which was proof she was too young for that. Like any two women living in the same household, they got their periods at about the same time, and every month Cerise would find in the wastebasket reassurance that Sophie's period had come too.

You have to be careful now, Cerise said.

Don't worry, Sophie said. I'm not going to end up wiping butts my whole life.

She could learn how to make a bed with someone in it. Easy to do if you first creased the sheets correctly. After Cerise scooched the patient to the right side of the bed, she tugged the flat sheet loose from the left side of the mattress and folded it over itself lengthwise, at intervals of one foot, pressing it flat each time. Hand over hand, she opened the oblong of the clean sheet to the length of the bed. Following the creases that ran in the perpendicular direction, she unfolded this sheet in the wake of the other until she reached the middle of the bed. Then she carefully hefted the patient onto the clean sheet. Some of them were so light she thought they would crumble in her hands. Some were plump as pigeons, dense, bunkered in their flesh. Cerise had a tolerance for the complaints that announced in advance the aches a shift would cause in tender joints, a cancerous gut, fresh surgical scars. After she moved the patient, she could strip the old sheet in one motion and then resume the slow unfolding of the new sheet. When she tucked the corners, she creased them twice so they'd fit under the mattress without lumps. The top sheet she unfurled like a sail so that it settled gently on the person in the bed.

She could croon an angry old man into holding still for a sponge bath, intimacy to which both of them must submit. The first few times Cerise gave Mr. Petersen a sponge bath, he smacked a fist on the basin of water and soaked the bed. She had to change the sheets later anyway, and he had a right to be angry: why did you have to continue to care for the body, long after its offerings had dwindled to punishment and humiliation? If his mind was weak, he was recovering well from his surgery, not like Mrs. Campos down the hall, who had an infected abscess in her jaw, packed with two feet of gauze tape that soaked up blood and pus and had to be unspooled and replaced every day. It made no difference. It made no difference that this one's children came every weekend and that one's children did not. It made no difference that this one would pass soon and that one might spend years in the same dim room, with the dusty blinds serrating the light from the narrow window. All of them hid in their fists some last little thing they could not yet give up. Cerise got Mr. Petersen to yield to her by degrees, let him soap himself at first, knowing his body would outmaneuver his will, not with its power to punish but with its hunger for relief. She had to hold his hand to lift his arm for washing, and he wanted someone to hold his hand. When she drew the soapy sponge over the pouching skin of his chest, the ridged scar on his belly, the furred and knotted muscle of his thigh, the steel-wool bristle of his pubic hair, she swaddled him in a haze of tenderness, oh honey, oh sweetie, almost done. Even wasted flesh wanted that tender touch.

Cerise had practice at the patience she needed once Sophie turned sixteen; her marvel of a girl woke up one day to rail as if all along she'd been waiting for the chance to lodge a complaint, and when Cerise came back from work she'd better hear it and not flinch. Not flinch, even when she got home late after seeing the podiatrist about her bunions and Sophie hadn't even started dinner.

Sophie really got going when they sat down to their meal of Stouffer's macaroni and cheese: My English teacher wants us to write a paper on how we can relate to Hamlet's confusion about life, and we have to use real examples. The teachers are such ghouls, prying into your personal life, and if you want to get an A, you have to spill your guts. And my math teacher puts new problems on the board and says, I bet even Sophie can't figure out this one, because he's got to show he still knows more than I do. I'm required by law to spend eight hours with these people, and then I get to go to work, where I can rub shoulders with some really brilliant types. You get these customers who hand you a dozen coupons, and if you tell them it's only the fourteen-ounce bottle of conditioner and not the thirty-two-ounce bottle that's on sale, they wave the coupon at you like it's the Magna Carta. It says so right here! Right here!

Whenever Cerise interrupted to ask a question (Wasn't this the English teacher Sophie liked? Couldn't she write a paper about something else? What was the Magna Carta?), Sophie said, You never let me finish a sentence. You never listen.

Even Jackson couldn't escape Sophie's scorn. Sophie said, He comes over this afternoon with his dog, and he says he could kill the dog with his bare hands, and he wants me to bet him, he'd do it for twenty bucks, and I'm, like, yeah, Jackson, I would be so impressed.

I don't want you alone here with him, Cerise said.

Why? What do you think will happen?

You get the dishes tonight, Cerise said. I'm on my feet all day.

Sophie said, I have homework.

My feet are so bad, the doctor says I have to have surgery. You didn't even start dinner before I came home.

Sophie held an imaginary violin under her chin and pretended to draw a bow across it. I'm on my feet all day, and I come home to slave over a meal, and my selfish daughter doesn't even care how I'm suffering.

I didn't say that, Cerise said.

Yes you did. You know just how to say it.

Cerise got up from the table. I don't want to argue, she said.

But Sophie followed her from the kitchen to the living room and back again. Sophie wanted her to admit she was in the wrong. Cerise took her cigarettes and went out to the landing on the back stairs, where only one person could fit, and Sophie opened the kitchen window and stuck her head out and kept at her. Cerise was such a coward she wouldn't even say why she didn't want Jackson in the house, and she didn't have any reason not to like him, and she was warping Sophie, warping her, by not trusting her.

Cerise went back inside and past Sophie to the bathroom, where she locked the door. Sophie thumped frantically on the door, yelling at her. Cerise let the water run in the sink, so the sound would drown out Sophie's voice. She tried not to smoke in the house, but if Sophie would not leave her in peace on the landing, then she could sit on the edge of the bathtub and light another cigarette.

Sophie finally went away. But she came back. She pushed slips of paper under the door, torn from one of her school notebooks.

Cerise knew it would be more of the same written on those pieces of paper, and still she laughed. Just picture Sophie at the table, tongue between her teeth, her hand zigzagging furiously across the page. Sophie had transformed herself from the relentless creature at the door into a daughter who could not let go. Cerise felt giddy, the way she did when one of the boys came to visit. She imagined them sometimes, grown men, making their annual trek to her door, bearing gifts more lavish than she could ever have wished for.

＊ ＊ ＊ ＊ ＊

Girls went through a phase of hating their mothers.

Sophie was so smart, Cerise didn't have to worry when she found
the marijuana tucked inside a sock in her daughter's top drawer,
when her daughter brought home a scruffy man of twenty who
might pocket her virginity but could never outwit Sophie's
careful plans for college, when her daughter tried to badger her
into screaming back. The day Cerise found the dope, she knew
she was looking in the wrong place for the wrong thing: if she
found a disk of birth control pills, there'd be no point in warning
Sophie to be careful with that boy, would there? Cerise waited a
few weeks before she spoke to Sophie. She asked her if she had
ever tried marijuana, if there was pressure from the other kids.
Sophie said, *You* smoke. Cerise did not know what to say to that,
how to make Sophie behave like a scolded child.

Sophie didn't always badger her; sometimes on Friday nights
they still rented a video and pulled out the sofa bed and banged
their heels on the mattress and hollered, No one can make me do
nothing! Nothing! And that Thursday night, they were having a
good time. Sophie had made golden tofu for dinner and brought
home from work some moleskin pads for Cerise's bunions. She
had washed the dishes before she started her homework. Cerise
was in the living room, ironing her uniform, when Sophie called
from the bedroom for her to come quick.

This spider was a big one, high up on the wall, and Cerise had
to stand on the bed to squish it. Its plump body crunched under
her finger, leaving a rusty smear on the wall. Sophie screamed.
She wanted proof the spider was dead. Cerise had to show her
the flattened body on the paper towel before she threw it into

the overflowing wastebasket in the bathroom. Sophie said she would not be able to sleep in her bed tonight if Cerise did not clean the stain, so Cerise got some disinfectant from the kitchen and sponged from the wall all those invisible eggs.

Now wash your hands, Sophie said. Wash your hands!

Sophie followed Cerise to the kitchen to watch her wash her hands, and then she followed her back to the living room. Thank you, Mom. Thanks.

Her patients thanked Cerise all the time. Mrs. Anderson tried to give her a silver-framed mirror, and another woman was always offering her fruit from a little bowl on her nightstand, peaches and apples with puckered skin that would soften to pulp in Cerise's pocket. Out of gratitude, these people confided little secrets, complaints and sorrows that were not the ones that mattered: *I met my husband right after the war, and you know I thought he was ugly the first time I saw him. Poppy would belt me if he caught me, so I said it was my sister did it. I embroidered these handkerchiefs myself, and I want you to have them before those others steal them on me.* Cerise always listened; she had learned early on in her nursing career that you could pinch the arm of someone suffering from a slipped disk and momentarily trick the brain out of feeling the agony by provoking the nerves elsewhere.

Sophie stood too close to Cerise at the ironing board, crowding her.

What? Cerise said. What is it?

Jackson wants me to go to school here. Or go to community college with him—he's thinking of starting. He wants us to stay together.

A shame you mailed off all those applications, Cerise said. Wrote all those checks.

Sophie sneered. You're so hopeless at this. So transparent.

Cerise had to nudge Sophie to get her to stand back. You have anything you want me to press while I've got the iron out?

You don't have to wait on me.

You bring me a few things.

Sophie went to her room and brought back some blouses and two pairs of jeans. Thanks, Mom. Thanks.

Honey, Cerise said. Do you love him?

Sometimes. Sophie heaved a great sigh, the kind of sigh for which she would pounce on Cerise. Sometimes he's just someone I hooked up with in high school. Everybody knows that can't last. That's not how life works.

Cerise thought of how well the boys had turned out. With so little trouble.

She set down the iron and pulled her warm uniform from the ironing board, shaking it out before she slipped it on the hanger.

I want you to be happy, Cerise said. I always want that.

I think I'm pregnant, Sophie said.

One day Cerise and Sophie would be friends again, and don't think of it. Cerise put down the iron when Sophie said she thought she might be pregnant. Sophie waited. Then she said, So now what?

The desire to retaliate flashed in Cerise, so strong. She knew she should not speak.

She went out onto the landing. She felt vindicated for not giving up a month of cigarettes so Sophie could send off another application. Sophie had made her sit down to fill in the financial aid forms, sign here, here, here, and Cerise had hesitated each time, because if she didn't concentrate she might mess up

Sophie's neat pages, and she must have gotten up from the table and come out here a dozen times that night so she wouldn't cry. That was the point of smoking. For so long as you drew on a cigarette, you did not care. Whatever kind of chemistry produced that comfort, it worked. Your mind did not course ahead of you—*so now what?*—but relished the sinkhole of the present, translated even misery to grim satisfaction. A *thank you* was all it took for Sophie to sucker Cerise. Oh, and the rush to kill the spider, to do one thing for Sophie that she could not do better for herself. So Sophie wouldn't have to shudder at the sight, Cerise had pushed the crumpled paper towel down into the overstuffed wastebasket. Now she meditated on that mess. Thick packets, wadded with toilet paper. Squeamish Sophie wrapped her sanitary napkins over and over again to seal off what they contained.

Cerise was afraid she would give out on Sophie. Like maybe she had only so many years of mothering in her, and she'd signed on for a job she did not have the heart to finish. She did not want to wonder why her daughter would tell her such a vicious lie any more than she wanted to know why Sophie was afraid of spiders. Instead of trying not to think about it, Sophie searched for reasons to cement her dread. She went on the Internet and reported to Cerise: there was a spider in Australia the size of a dinner plate, and it ate birds, and what would you do if you were walking along and one dropped on you from a tree; another spider laid its eggs in the bodies of the insects it trapped in its web, so the babies could feed on the host when they hatched.

When Cerise came inside, Sophie had taken her place at the ironing board and was running the iron over her blouse, wrinkling the fabric because she did not know to tug the cuff so the sleeve would not crease.

Let me do that, Cerise said.

Reflex for Cerise to take the iron from Sophie and patiently start over on the blouse. Instinct to take comfort from the young body so close beside her she could smell the lavender conditioner in Sophie's hair, see the fine down at her jawline, long to submit to the easy generosity one body could summon from another and lie down inside her daughter's wishes with her.

Again Sophie waited for Cerise to say something.

Cerise finished the sleeve and began running the iron over the front of the blouse, steering it in and out between the buttons.

You're not pregnant, Cerise said.

What would you know about it? Sophie said. When did you ever have the satisfaction?

She stood so brutally close. *Lie down with me here.*

You get yourself tangled up with him, Cerise said. What will you get for it? He's not going to college in the fall. He's not going ever. He's not fit for you. You think he doesn't know that? You think he doesn't know nothing attached to him can get very far?

Sophie tugged at the shirt.

But Cerise would not lift the iron. A burning smell rose from the fabric.

Cerise watched the cloth begin to brown.

Sophie watched too, her hand suspended in air, as if she had no choice but to stand there.

Mama, she said softly, you'll ruin it.

When Cerise finally lifted the iron to set it upright, there was her daughter's hand, still hovering, and she swung the iron so its tip would just kiss that outstretched hand. The iron spit when it came in contact with the warm, moist flesh.

Sophie didn't cry out. She gripped her wrist and held her hand before her as if she had to study the triangular imprint the iron had left, erasing the crisscrossing lines on the skin of her palm, searing a fresh new blank, a clean slate.

Scissors, Paper, Rock

These days the staff treated Natalie like a family retainer who had faltered long ago but was kept on, given occasional tasks and told nostalgic lies about her continuing usefulness. Little else remained of the paper's beginnings as an alternative weekly, precariously surviving from issue to issue. It had evolved into a chain of regional papers with a steady advertising income, carefully niched to avoid competing with San Francisco's daily paper. Natalie continued to collect a small monthly check, a kill fee, and visited the office every few weeks. Though she had chopped off her long hair, she still dressed in the same careless way, sexy black, but slightly out-of-date and vaguely mournful on a woman well past fifty, and the dash of red lipstick had begun to look more like evidence of incompetence and less like the afterthought of someone who didn't need to bother. She might still get her feet under her again, and now and then she turned in a photograph they could use. No one minded if she showed up and closeted herself in the tiny darkroom, appropriating whatever supplies she needed.

Just an oversight that one day when she came in, the receptionist barred her way. Holly was new. She was insisting that Natalie could not use the copier unless she had been issued a copier card, and she would have to leave her dog outside, when Liz interrupted her. Liz introduced them—Holly in a hot pink tank top and denim skirt, Natalie dressed in her usual black—and explained that exceptions were made for Natalie. Her little gray poodle was OK too. Charlie trotted after Natalie and curled up politely at her feet when she stopped at the copier. Liz swiped her own magnetic card—to hand it over to Natalie was to forfeit it—but could not leave her by herself.

Natalie needed Liz to tell her how to select a paper tray so she could copy onto ledger-sized paper.

I have to document my claims, she said.

This couldn't be more paperwork for the house; she had sold it a year ago, just after her divorce. Doc was hardly the love of her life—she'd flamed out on lovers long before he appeared on the scene and she decided to take refuge—and it was not a messy breakup. No one had expected it to derail Natalie. At work she reported a series of afflictions: the run-down house, riddled with dry rot and mortgaged to the hilt, had to be sold at a loss; she could not find a landlord who would permit a dog; her battered old car was stolen; in her new neighborhood she was mugged; she no longer went out alone at night after that. Maybe no one read any of this very accurately. Just after Natalie and Doc broke up, the World Trade Center went up in flames, stunning everyone and inaugurating a long, uncertain wait. What was coming in the wake of this catastrophe? At work they installed a TV and kept it tuned to CNN, MSNBC, any twenty-four-hour news programming; Natalie alone lost interest in images, turning in fewer and fewer photographs. People at the office began saying maybe something was wrong.

Liz showed Natalie how to use the touch pad to specify the dimensions of the copy she was making.

Natalie thought this was miraculous. But worrisome too.

I bet we'll all be neurologically rewired in another generation, she said. Nothing is done manually. Even in art school the students aren't taught to use their hands anymore. And these digital cameras. No mistake is ever real, because you clean up the image on the computer screen before you print it. If you bother to print. I'll be the last one still using the darkroom.

Liz laughed. You already are.

When Liz started here as a paste-up artist, each issue was laid out on blue-lined grid paper taped to light boards bolted to the walls; you walked around the room with an x-acto blade, trimming sheets of paper—text, headlines, ads, and halftones—that had been rolled through a hot waxer to back them with a sticky coat of paraffin. Now she supervised two designers who did all the work on a template at the computer and transmitted electronic files to the printer's offices. Raised on the striptease of MTV jump cuts, Josh and Ashley dressed, like Holly, in jarring colors, hot pink and chartreuse and lemon yellow, and they couldn't hide their dismay at sacrificing their cutting-edge ideas to the dubious priority of readable text. Liz existed to tamp their high spirits, the mommy who always said no.

Natalie sifted through the papers she had copied. Legal documents, she said. My landlord is trying to evict me. When I thought he was such a nice man. It's so hard to be a grown-up. I have to fend him off, and then the neighbors too. They don't like Charlie. I can't leave him home. I'm afraid they'll try to poison him.

Liz almost wished that some nasty neighbor had actually made threats. Like everyone else here, Liz wanted to be kind, to extend a generosity that presumed so much room in which to drift, so much cushion for a fall. But what if Natalie was about to crash and burn?

Josh and Ashley had been the first to figure out that Natalie no longer floated harmlessly through the office. Mostly, food went missing. Stashes of cookies from desk drawers, sandwiches from the fridge in the lunchroom. A box of sugar packets. A thermos of iced tea. The thermos was replaced in the kitchen a few weeks later. She must be hungry, Josh said. Ashley, full of eager pity, deliberately left jars of peanut butter and loaves of bread on the counter in the lunchroom. They had not known Natalie before, and their charitable impulses came unencumbered.

When Liz was just a part-timer on the paste-up crew, she resented Natalie. They'd have the layout up on the wall, gaping holes awaiting Natalie's photographs, and Natalie would be in the darkroom still developing negatives or sitting on the editor's desk discussing whether she should get the cover. Once she delivered the photo, Natalie studied the layout, worrying that the page should be torn up and redone, soliciting advice from Rick, the layout editor then. Hesitantly, as if she regretted the professional judgment that held her back from easy acquiescence, she would touch his wrist and wonder *but what if*, and he would linger a little longer.

People gossiped about it. Natalie got away with holding up the show because (1) she'd slept with just about every male whose name was on the masthead, and (2) she was hustling her past glory for all it was worth. Her star was already fading, but she had helped to make the name of the paper, had even been nominated for a national prize for a series of photos she'd done as the Vietnam War was winding down. She freelanced for a wire service as well and could easily have made better money working elsewhere full-time, but she had remained loyal.

They worked until they put the issue to bed, and the consequence of Natalie's indecision might be hours of delay. It made a difference to Liz to go home at midnight instead of nine or ten. She got up with the kids at six every morning. She worked weekends and Fridays, when Denny could leave work early to fetch Leah from preschool and Nick from kindergarten. They needed the money and Denny was already sacrificing himself, working in corporate public relations and coming home to do dishes and give the kids baths. She was underemployed pasting up ads—a clean visual reconfigured from scrawled copy and a hasty sketch submitted by the sales reps—but she craved time with her kids, wanted to make the sacrifice, to be a throwback.

Liz would have gone on resenting Natalie, but one night when she rapped on the darkroom door to urge her to hurry up, Natalie let her into the red light of the room and apologized as she swished the paper in the developing fluid with a pair of tongs. Her lush black hair, which fell to her waist, was pinned back with one of the clothespins they used to hang drying prints.

Natalie pulled up a stool for Liz and handed her the still gummy proof sheet and a magnifying lens. She wanted Liz to choose the best shot. She seemed oblivious that she had a dozen years' experience on Liz, a lowly paste-up artist.

The photos had been taken to accompany a story on the

AIDS ward at San Francisco General. Instead of shooting doctors and nurses ministering to cadaverous patients, Natalie had photographed people flipping through magazines in the waiting room, a smiley-face sticker on a stethoscope, a receptionist studying an appointment ledger with its penciled-over cancellations. She had a knack for locating the most intense point of focus at the periphery of the frame.

These are really good, Liz said.

People aren't wary around me, Natalie said. That's it. My only secret.

Nothing here is the obvious choice, Liz said.

You don't think it's too much—too much *a woman's eye?* Natalie said. The human story instead of the hard facts? Because you know that's what they like to use me for. Get a girl to do the soft stuff. I'm pushing forty. I'd like to break out of that box. And then again I wouldn't.

We could talk for a long time about a woman's eye, Liz said.

It's like intermittent reinforcement, Natalie said. They want you to behave like a man at work. Except every once in a while they don't.

That gave them a lot to talk about. Liz had discovered that when she proofread the ads, she caught more errors than anyone else, saving the paper hundreds of dollars a month in rebates to advertisers. She'd screwed up her courage to ask for a raise. And then when she started pushing for health benefits for part-time staff—mostly women—her boss wanted to know why the raise wasn't enough for her.

She said, And I won't lie when I have to stay home from work because of a sick kid.

Oh, you have *babies*, Natalie said.

They never think you know your own worth, Liz said.

You've got me beat on every front, Natalie said. Marriage and kids, that takes real guts. Of course you figured this out already, but I only just realized you can't go on having boyfriends forever. Doc's a steady guy. He does actual work for a living, and now I have a roof over my head. But it's kind of an experiment, living with a man. I still don't feel married.

Someone else had to come rap on the door to fetch Liz. How easily Natalie could pull you aside from whatever you were doing, make you forget you had to get back to it.

Liz changed into her walking shoes, pulled her iPod from her drawer, and clipped it to her belt. She would stop at the managing editor's desk on her way out for her lunch-hour walk. The missing food had come up at their editorial meeting, but no one had known what to do: maybe just accept the tithe Natalie exacted? Searching in the back files, Liz had hit upon a new strategy. She'd found a folder with Natalie's photographs of Vietnam vets, taken at Hamilton Air Force Base, at a time when Liz was still in school and Natalie couldn't have been more than twenty. Then, images of combat flickered on the TV set every day, sudden proliferation, the first war telecast into the living rooms of ordinary Americans. Natalie had met the flights of soldiers returning from a tour of duty. Some men came back in pressed uniforms and severe crew cuts; others tied bandannas over their raggedy hair. Natalie's photographs delineated what you knew you could not see, whether and how the war would rage on in any of those men.

Their chain of papers rarely covered national news—local listings mattered more to their readers than such hubris—but soon the Bush administration would take its case to the United Nations, press for war on Iraq. In the next issue they could print the photos instead of some shrill condemnation.

Liz stopped at Rick's office door to float her proposal, headphones yoked around her neck.

Rick pushed his chair back from his desk and waved her in, but she stayed where she was. If she sat down, he'd put his feet on the desk to emphasize that they were just chatting, no pulling rank here. Endearing, except when she needed a simple yes or no.

Liz said that if they reprinted Natalie's photos, they could kill two birds with one stone.

Rick shrugged. We can screw a magnetic reader to the lunch room door so you have to swipe your ID card to get in. Problem solved.

You're missing the point, Liz said.

Which is what? Rick said. To make sure Natalie feels the love? That's not going to keep ham sandwiches from flying out of the refrigerator.

Maybe we should call social services, Liz said.

She can't need welfare. She must still have some money left from the sale of the house.

Liz said, I was thinking psychiatric evaluation.

Whoa! Rick said. Let's go back to the hippie option.

What if she really needs help?

She's always been a little off, Rick said. And she's muddled through. Maybe someone could just talk to her.

A chat. Liz refused to take the bait.

You're the one with the big ideas, he said.

Outside Liz jammed on her headphones and turned up the volume, rock music she couldn't indulge in around Denny because he was such a snot about pop culture. Why didn't Denny have the guts to sneer at her music instead of pretending it bewildered him? Why did Rick think Liz should be the one to talk to Natalie? Because she was the only woman — still — on senior staff. Because maybe these guys couldn't handle the intimate difficulties of humiliating a woman they once desired. Because *feel the love,* crouched inside this show of virtuous tolerance was a bunch of cowards. And she must be one too, her vigilance just another dodge.

On her walks Liz thought long and hard and unreliably: she had planned more than once to leave an unsuspecting Denny, right down to deciding which of their furniture to keep; persuaded herself that editorial had nothing but contempt for design at the newspaper and picked out a new career as a preschool teacher; burned with regret for the years she had stayed home with her children, only to have her fifteen-year-old daughter chafe at her mommyness, her hovering, and her son feel so relaxed and cozy he had yet to fill out any of the college applications due in a few months. Now she imagined Rick, feet up on his desk, watching her bounce around his office like a rubber ball, waiting for the frigging laws of thermodynamics to drain her trajectory of its force. Oh, she scared herself, thinking furiously, pumping her arms, braceleted with weights, to the driving beat of the music.

✦ ✦ ✦ ✦ ✦

Once in a while Natalie used to invite Liz and Denny to her dinner parties. Bring the babies, Natalie said. Generous about the kids in a way few childless people were, she stood them on chairs so they could help in the kitchen, and she tied her dog on the back porch so he wouldn't knock them over. In those days she owned a big, inconvenient dog. Liz had loved the charmed disarray of Natalie's run-down Victorian house: the plaster walls always in some stage of disrepair, the narrow rooms crammed with old furniture Natalie had refinished, mismatched chairs lined up at the scarred mahogany table, every available surface jammed with Japanese paperweights and clay animals from Mexico that Liz's children were allowed to touch. Natalie did the cooking and Doc did the dishes, and the children would have to be fed long before Natalie managed to bring a meal to the table, cassoulet, custards in ramekins, curries with homemade chutneys and raisins and freshly grated coconut. Natalie was up and down and up and down during these hours-long meals, fetching something else from the kitchen for her guests. Doc liked to say that he had to wash every dish in the house after a dinner party and Natalie had to sleep twelve hours to recover.

You never knew who'd show up at dinner. A guy running for the state assembly, a very bad painter married to a very good sculptor, a dean at the medical school, a guitar player. And sometimes Natalie's plumber or the woman next door. Never any other children because Liz's kids were THE children to Natalie, the first and only of their kind. She had a lot of questions for them and meant to extract their wisdom. In her house Liz was less vigilant, didn't worry when and what Nick and Leah ate or watch the clock, yet she found herself adopting

Natalie's solicitude toward her children. If Leah fretted because she'd smeared sticky sauce all over her face and hands, Liz would whisk her to the kitchen, Natalie following on her heels, to make a production of cleaning her up. Oh, she remembered this: plopping Leah on the counter by the sink, legs dangling, and Natalie handing her a wet washcloth, then a dish towel, as intent as a nurse in surgery. Natalie saying, It must be better than any love affair, but what a position to be in, because how can you not want to depend on some man to stand in the doorway so you can be safe inside with this, and we don't really need them for much else, maybe to drive you places because driving always makes me a little afraid. You had to smile at that, but plucking Leah from the counter, Liz felt tears stinging her eyes, mysterious upwelling.

After they arrived home and tucked away their sleeping children, Denny would say to Liz, Doc seems happy enough, but I couldn't live with her. They would crawl into bed and talk over everything: Doc's indulgent willingness to let Natalie preside at the table; whether or not Natalie might be sleeping with that painter—the two of them had disappeared into the kitchen to whip cream for dessert, for too long, and when they returned he'd sat quietly dabbing at the flecks of cream spattered on his shirt, not looking up—and if Doc had made some bargain or suffered over this; the profligacy of Natalie's meals, so of a piece with the way she had squandered her early success, when she must have had plenty of offers coming in; how much their children trusted Natalie—Leah had sat in her lap at dinner and Nick had delicately flicked the tiny switches of the Leica she blithely handed him. In their retelling, regretfully, Liz and Denny folded their children back into their ordinary size, and

Liz would say she dreaded Leah waking up in the morning, expecting to be waited on. In bed together they remembered exactly who and where they were, murmuring, pressed against each other's warm skin.

Once again Josh and Ashley caught on before everyone else. They liked to work late just before a deadline—to pretend they were slaving at some start-up in Silicon Valley—and one night as they were leaving, they saw Natalie's car, door ajar while Charlie scrambled out to pee at the curb. If Josh had thought first, he would not have sneaked up to the car to get a look in the window, setting off the dog and scaring Natalie. She was sleeping in the car.

The two of them could not let her into the offices because she would trigger the newly installed alarm; the editors had refused to move from their original location in Portrero Hill, despite a series of break-ins, despite the eerie emptiness of the warehouse district at night, despite everyone's prevailing consciousness of security. Natalie declined Ashley's offer of her sofa for the night. Impulsive creatures but not truly careless, the kids never considered the possibility that Natalie sleeping in her car was none of their business.

No satisfaction for Liz in this vindication of her suspicions. Maybe Natalie had slept in her car just that one night, for some approximately plausible reason. Maybe Liz had changed, not Natalie. Maybe Natalie would have muddled on if Liz hadn't wished this curse on her. Rick should be the one to talk to Natalie, Rick with his healthier, lazier sense of circumspection. But he called Liz once he'd coaxed Natalie into his office. Hey, why don't you drop on by?

Rick had his feet up on his desk when Liz arrived, and Natalie sat facing him, Charlie curled in her lap. Natalie's hair was sleek, and if her long black skirt was dowdy, it was neat and unwrinkled. She didn't look as if she had been sleeping in a car. Liz raised a hand to smooth her own hair. Vanity, as much as efficacy, sent her out to pound the pavement on her lunch hour. If she couldn't pull off the screaming flags of color worn by her arty staff, she was trim at forty-five and could wear clothes well.

Natalie smiled at her. The landlord changed my locks. Boom! Out on the street, and I don't even know what became of my furniture. So I've been desperately reading the classifieds.

Natalie waved at the sheet of newsprint on Rick's desk, proof. You know how hard it is to find a place that will take pets? And I've never been good at things like this. I can't even balance a checkbook.

Natalie crossed her legs and leaned conspiratorially toward Rick. Do you remember when I used to have to fill in expense reports?

Rick grinned. You attached receipts for pantyhose because you couldn't find the stub for gas or whatever, and you didn't see why we'd fuss over details.

Liz tried to catch Rick's eye, to lodge some protest, but he had forgotten her presence. Josh had told her the car was stuffed with junk, shoeboxes and books and bags of clothes. Natalie could not have been summarily locked out.

I consider pantyhose a legitimate business expense, Natalie said. *You* try clambering on scaffolding to get a clear shot of some politician at a rally, and see if you wouldn't snag your hose on a screw.

Natalie's hands moved over the dog with hypnotic smooth- .

ness. There was no pressing crisis. There was never anything pressing with Natalie. How many times had she tugged Rick over to stare forever at a layout with a photo that really could be cropped more effectively? A lot of the freelance photographers Liz used now didn't even bother to deliver proof sheets; they e-mailed her a JPEG file. They didn't fuss over which photo she chose; it was just work, competently tossed off.

Rick scanned the classified page for possibilities. You can use my phone to call some of these places, he told Natalie.

Could you—I don't always know one neighborhood from another, Natalie said. If you could just star the ones you think I should look at. Where I'm not going to end up in some junkie hotel.

He already had a pen in his hand, happy to supply the competence Natalie divined in others.

The dog moaned with pleasure under Natalie's languorous hands.

Sometimes I don't know what possesses people, she said. To just lock me out. Why wouldn't you talk to someone first? I can't help feeling hurt.

I'll keep my eyes open for you, Rick said. You wouldn't know of a place for rent, would you, Liz?

Liz knew lots of people. She and Denny had friends who'd bought two- or three-unit places to rent out, were considering investing their money in the same way, now that they were making a decent living. Mentally she began listing apartments that might be available, industriousness kicking right in. I could make some calls, she said.

She couldn't help feeling scammed.

Why had Liz and Denny stopped going to dinner at Natalie's? She had gradually withdrawn into a quiet semi-retirement, where there were no more flagrant flirtations, fewer and fewer of the lavish dinner parties. The kids began to chafe at sitting through adult parties; they wanted to be with their friends. Natalie wasn't always careful when they were around and Liz didn't like having to explain away the dope smoke drifting in from her back porch. The kids got older, and Liz could revel in this era of their competence and her own, finally devote herself to her career. At last Denny could quit his hated job. They could afford to take a gamble; he started his own public relations business, recruiting nonprofits and arts organizations as clients, and for a while their lives were a precarious balancing act, hewing to a vexing budget, frantically bartering over which of them would drive the kids to soccer practice, tossing dinners on the table. But Denny was making a go of it, and Liz got the promotion to art director, and their kids grew sound and sturdy, and their life together was charged with a striving vitality.

By then Natalie was working only one assignment at a time for the newspaper, even though she'd given up work for the wire service—she didn't like to travel. The paper had switched to using computers for layout, and though Natalie tried to muster some curiosity, sitting at Liz's desk for a demonstration, she marveled at Liz's adaptability and said if she were Liz, she would just go home with a headache. She still wanted Liz's opinion, but not as an egalitarian gesture. Natalie could no longer wander through a busy paste-up room to halt their progress with her tentative inquiries, because everything was done piecemeal by people working alone. But when she showed up to deliver an assignment, work halted, as if for an important visitor who could not be expected to register how she disrupted their day. People turned their backs to their desks and settled in to talk to her. She brought Rick a bag of fresh apricots from her own tree and sat in his office eating one of them while editorial assistants came and went with copy, and she needed him to dab a Kleenex to her juice-stained face. He did it out of gallantry: her flesh had settled in a pouchy, middle-aged way even if her manners were not subject to the inroads of gravity.

When Natalie dropped by Liz's office, Liz learned to listen patiently while part of her mind churned through a list of things to do. Natalie's visits reminded her of the happy time when her children were small, and they taught her over and over how to let each day happen as it would, centered on the wobbly axis of their needs and not her own intentions. The sick days that disrupted her plans were also enticing pools of time in which she might spend an entire afternoon reading in bed with a feverishly hot child pressed against her or playing endless rounds of scissors, paper, rock, in which no strategy could defeat the illogic of the hierarchy that set paper over rock, an open hand over a fist.

One day, in her soft, doubting way, Natalie told Liz that it seemed Doc was leaving her. Natalie, who'd damaged a few marriages in her time, had abruptly lost her subdued consort to a younger woman.

But I'm taking it well, she said.

Don't be nice! Liz said. Throw something at him when he comes by to pick up his stuff.

Natalie smiled, delighted, and then shook her head. Doc has been good to me.

Liz said, At least get a decent lawyer and kick his butt in court.

Natalie shook her head again. Doc's been so considerate about the money. He offered me a percentage of his retirement fund. I don't have any right to it. I never paid any attention to things like pensions. I'll be OK if we can get a good price for the house. He's going to help me invest my share.

Doc's lawyer buried her in legal documents she couldn't decipher. She could not remember to pay her utility bills and had to deliver money orders in person to get her lights and gas turned back on. But she seemed merely perplexed by the string of misfortunes that followed on her divorce, as if this accrued interest on her fecklessness had missed its aim. When her car was stolen, she discovered she had failed to renew her auto insurance. After the car was retrieved, dumped in a parking lot by the kids who'd taken it for a joyride, Natalie photographed what she found in it—candy wrappers, a charm bracelet, a CD still in its shrink-wrap, empty soda cans—and marveled that these kids had also left a receipt that could have been traced back to them, as if they had stolen the car only so she could discover their identity and wonder.

They had snatched Natalie back from the lip of the precipice. Liz tapped all her resources to find an attic apartment with decent light; Rick cajoled Josh and Ashley into helping him paint the rooms (don't let them choose the colors, Liz warned); they retrieved Natalie's possessions from her former landlord, who agreed to forgo ransoming them for back payment of rent. Masses of junk, Ashley reported, all these little tchotchkes just tossed into cartons.

A host of plans seemed suddenly viable to Liz. After the paper recycled Natalie's photos of Vietnam vets, Liz might be able to find a gallery to host an exhibit of her photographs. She could draw on Denny's connections with clients at arts organizations, lean on her own contacts in the media, try to get a feature article. Easy to imagine what a good story Natalie would make now. More interesting than deciding on the layout for this week's column on postmodern etiquette. *Q: Given these times of heightened airport security, is it inadvisable to pack in one's suitcase a modest amount of marijuana for recreational purposes?*

Liz was glad to see Natalie the next time she dropped by her office, thinking how many gifts she might still proffer. Natalie was turning in an assignment on time for once, still buoyed, and she wanted Liz to look at the proof sheet. She had been sent to cover a street fair in the Mission, but she'd taken a little liberty with the assignment.

I trust your opinion, Natalie said.

Liz didn't bother to scope the proof sheet with the magnifying lens. Natalie had photographed a sewer lid, a serrated foil gum wrapper plastered against a fence, a tattered streamer wrapped like a boa around a streetlamp. Available light was superbly managed in each black-and-white photo, shadows a grainy, rich register of grays, each object crisply outlined. Only the tattered streamer bore any connection to the street fair Natalie had been asked to cover.

It's probably wrong, Natalie said. I've been thinking other people must feel this way. Your field of vision just jammed with things screaming for your attention. You end up—you can't look. You couldn't nail that with one photo. You'd have to take a bunch that were all missing the same thing. What you can't look at.

Some urgent impulse fired up in Liz, the way that it would when Natalie, sorting her divorce papers, refused to get mad.

Where's the damn street fair? she said.

I knew it was a gamble, Natalie said softly. I should never be left to my own devices.

Liz wanted to plead: you could try.

But Josh came by with a question, and Natalie needed to thank him again for painting her walls and ask about his weekend and approve of his participation in the protest march on Sunday. Liz had gone to the march too. She and Denny had taken the subway downtown, kids in tow for a lesson in participatory democracy, and joined the placid crowd on Market Street. She read in the paper later that it was the largest U.S. protest against the war on Iraq, a war that hadn't started yet but seemed a fait accompli. There were mimes performing on street corners and a sea of homemade signs: NO BLOOD FOR OIL, A VILLAGE IN TEXAS IS MISSING ITS IDIOT. Liz had felt silly, dutiful yet out of place, giggling with her daughter about how this beat out all her other field trips and wincing for her son, rank amateur at knowingness, when he assured her this government wouldn't dare reinstate the draft. Next year he would have to register for it anyway.

After Natalie left, Josh poked around on Liz's desk until he discovered the proof sheet she'd left behind. Oh wow, he said, what a trip.

See if you can guess what her assignment was, Liz said.

These shots are *so* radical, Josh said. I *love* them. They *so* refuse to locate a subject. Maybe she's just ahead of the curve.

I don't want to hear it, Liz said.

He mistook this for another salvo in their debates over what constituted good design. Think outside the box! he urged.

Liz depended on Josh and Ashley—their hip taste, their alertness to trends—to counter the cautious sensibility authority imposed. In private, after she firmly insisted on changes to a layout, she had taken to second-guessing herself.

Later, when Liz stopped by his desk to drop off an assignment, she saw that Josh had scanned one of Natalie's proofs into the computer to use as a screen saver. The image of the foil gum wrapper, flattened against a fence, wavered on his screen, colorized so that it gleamed silver against the lurid aquamarine tint he had applied to the background.

Natalie was something in her heyday. She was. Somehow the myth had become as much a part of Liz's memory as witnessed fact. Liz, watching her in the paste-up room, hovering in a way that conjured gentle attentiveness, could believe there had been no bloodshed in all the love affairs attributed to her, no accusations on parting. Could see in the blowsy gestures of that slender woman the disarming charm that had housed, like a Trojan horse, the girl who'd made her reputation at twenty. She hadn't needed to be aggressive or reckless to get those shots of returning GIs at Hamilton Air Force Base. She hadn't needed to be ambitious or daring on the night of the Dan White riots when the killer of Mayor Moscone and Harvey Milk was acquitted of murder; she waited till the early hours of morning to capture a man seated on the hood of a squad car, staring at his cupped hands, the bashed windshield a cloudy sunburst behind him.

She hadn't needed to be calculating or clever to count among her friends famous artists and up-and-coming politicians who did not mind having a pretty girl in their circle and felt protective toward her freakish talent.

Liz came in to the office early one Thursday morning so she could work in peace; Josh and Ashley never showed up before nine. When she saw Natalie's car parked at the curb, she wanted to charge the car and rap on the window to scare Natalie awake. When we got you that nice apartment!

The backseat held evidence of Natalie's night—a bunched blanket, a pillow jammed against the door—but no Natalie. A sickening shift, fear caroming in Liz's chest.

Liz turned to scan the sidewalk. It took her a moment to recognize Natalie, all the way down at the corner. Standing too close to a man who loomed over her. One of the street people who lived around here. So easy to spot, even at this distance, the mashed hair, the layers of clothing, some aura of decay warping the air around him. Even Natalie's proximity to him betrayed the direction of her drift. Just look at her. The limp sack of her long skirt. The misapplied lipstick blurring her mouth.

The man had Natalie's dog footballed under one arm, and Natalie was hunched over her gaping purse, digging around in it, looking up every now and then to murmur what looked like apology.

The man jerked his head, scanning the sidewalk just as Liz had, taking her in as accurately and immediately as she'd slotted him. With his free hand he jabbed at Natalie's elbow. Liz hurried to reach them, *how to do what next* still churning, still driving her on.

She caught the last bit of the man's urgent coaxing. Come on, he said to Natalie, he's got to be worth more than that to you.

What are you doing? Liz demanded.

Both of them looked at her: startled, guilty, furtive. The man shifted his weight from one foot to the other, thrumming with readiness.

Oh, Natalie said. Oh, it's all right. Charlie got away from me and he caught him. He just wants a reward.

And she bent over her purse again, licking a thumb so she could sort the thick wad of bills in her hand, and even if they were all singles, it was too much money.

Give me the dog, Liz said. She reached for Charlie over the man's arm, and he adjusted his grip, and Liz could feel the frantic click of his calculations, to bash that arm into her chest or to let go of the dog, whichever proved the fastest way to what he wanted.

She couldn't move. Even when he jammed the dog into her waiting arms she couldn't do more than brace herself to accept the weight, locked in place while with one efficient motion he stripped the bills from Natalie's hand and swerved to make his escape.

Only the rush of air as he swept past Liz and broke into a run. She rocked like a boat at anchor.

She didn't doubt the good intentions of her colleagues or herself. But they had gotten so caught up in one commotion or another, throwing themselves into the sweet industry of rescue, the drama of the next escapade, as if the terrible moment would not transfix them when it came.

That's all he wanted, Natalie said. A reward.

She pulled a compact from the purse that still hung open on her arm, angling the mirror to examine her hair, reaching up to snag unruly strands. Of the beautiful, fluttering girl, only this artlessness remained.

A glimmering just out of reach.

Why don't you come inside? Liz said. Come in with me.

The Mechanics of Falling

Clay wakes up in the bathtub, naked. He pulls himself up on his elbows: he's bone dry and so is the tub, and his bass guitar is perched upright on the toilet seat. He could try to figure out how he got here, or he could stop at the reason slamming in his skull. He knows what woke him. Annie, banging a door somewhere in the house, as she does every morning. Sometimes he resigns himself and sometimes he gives her hell. When she first moved in, she used to pound him on the shoulder at 7:00 A.M. and hiss at him to come and watch her ride. To cure her of it, he picked her up one morning and dumped her on the porch and locked the door. She waited for him to come out and doused him with a bucket of water. Later he lay in wait for her with fistfuls of the warm mash they feed the horses. Then she found out he was afraid of snakes. The fields around the stables are full of them. Neither of them is ever going to cure the other.

He crawls out of the tub, rescues the guitar, and fishes a pair of jeans from the hamper. In the kitchen he finds Annie finishing a bowl of Lucky Charms, her hair already knotted in a braid that she can tuck under her riding helmet. She doesn't look up when he comes in, and he can't decide if her air of indifference stems from innocence or cunning.

He puts on coffee. She never does this for him, even though she's always up first. Probably that's too domestic. At first Annie was just a roommate. Letting her share the house on the property meant he could pay her less for helping him manage the barn and teaching a few lessons. That they ended up sleeping together was about as inevitable as the tit-for-tat escalation of their fights, and yet whenever he wakes to find her in his bed in the morning, he blinks in surprise. He's never sure it will happen again. It hasn't, not for a while.

Who took my clothes? he says.

You got your hands on a bottle of tequila.

Roger must have brought the bottle when he and Marty came over to play some music. One practice is so much like another, Clay can never remember too specifically. Maybe he blew out an amp again, and that's how his guitar ended up in the toilet. Maybe Marty got ticked off because Clay always tells him to shut up when he talks about getting another gig at the bar in town, where they played once for free beer.

Clay dips Annie's braid in her cereal bowl. Who took my clothes?

You shouldn't drink till you black out.

I seem to recall you had some tequila too.

I didn't wake up in the bathtub with no clothes on, she says.

I don't drink that much.

She considers this. No, you don't. Drinking's just your excuse. Why remember every stupid thing you did to end up like that when you can be amazed instead?

Clay can never just have a conversation with her. She's always ambitious to say something *real*, in a way that makes him able to imagine her in a college classroom not so long ago, raising her hand in answer to every question. She's too young for him. That first morning he woke up to find her staring back at him, skinny little Annie wrapped in his arms, she watched him try to work up the courage to speak and then she beat him to the punch. She smiled and said, Look what you got yourself into. Annie, I'm a fuckup, he began. She rolled out of bed and turned her back to him to put on a shirt. Yeah, I know, she said. She didn't let him finish. She didn't make him wriggle to get off the hook.

Annie takes her bowl to the sink. You can afford to pay me this month.

He pays her out of the cash box at the end of the week, and she takes whatever is left in it without complaint. Without even demanding an IOU. When she moved in with him, she had just dropped out of college and spent her last check from her parents on a horse. He can't figure her out. As a reward for turning twenty-one, she's about to come into some trust money from her grandmother, not a fortune, but a yearly check that will nicely fill out the gaps in his accounting. Now that she gets to have her cake and eat it too, she's decided to complain about her back pay.

I thought I didn't need to pay you anymore, he says.

I hate being young, she says. It doesn't matter how much you mean what you say. Everybody acts like they're in on the joke and you're not.

He finishes his coffee before he follows her outside. The barn and the paddocks are set smack up against rolling hills that frame the valley, and the trails behind the barn ascend through fields of parched grass and stands of live oak. But at his back, only faintly screened by trees, is a new subdivision of tasteful houses with cedar siding, the usual for Marin, and someday soon the trails will be sacrificed to another development. In ten years he's never worked at a barn that wasn't located in this between-space, not rural and not yet suburban.

Clay climbs onto the top rail of the fence so he can give Annie pointers while she trots Pablo around the arena. The horse came up lame last month, and he's still not sound enough to jump.

She was a fool to buy him. Because he is so big and broad in the chest, he wasn't much good at the racetrack, but for the same reason some sucker snapped him up at auction and trained him to jump, just in time for Annie to come along and think she saw a bargain, a horse with the build to take the punishment of eventing and the will to run. Then she rode him, and he acted like a punk. Sold. You keep a horse like that in his stall, trying to heal him up, and he's all piss and vinegar when you finally take him out, ready to hurt himself again at the first opportunity.

Clay yells at Annie to keep her heels down, lower her wrists, fucking use her outside rein on the half-halt. She'll take anything he dishes out when she's on horseback. The straight-A student who thinks she should be punished for not getting it perfect. That ought to spoil her as a rider, the same way all her little mistakes ought to matter. But she's got some second self that can disappear into the task and never look up from it. She's beautiful to watch: she looks as if her muscles have been lashed to the horse's spine.

When Clay plays bass with the guys, he feels the way she

looks, as if his fingers know how to do this without him, and he forgets the gap between what it feels like and the indifferent sound he must be producing.

Circling, Annie talks looking over her shoulder, one hand on the horse's rump. She says a horse in the paddock at the far end of the arena is knocking his feed bucket around, and Pablo has made up his mind to bolt whenever the bucket bangs the fence. He'll jump at any excuse. It's so cute.

Clay wishes she'd get over the girl-in-love stuff.

He orders her to move Pablo onto the rail and get him trotting.

When she asks for the canter, the horse explodes with a stiff-legged jump, and then he's bucking, a full-out rodeo performance. Annie sits him solidly, leaning back, heels down, her hands still, so light and unresisting he might forget she's on his back. Slowly, she gathers him in till he's trotting steadily, ears switching back and forth as if he is just itching for his next chance. She's biting her lip, but even that can't keep her from grinning.

Some people are too stupid to be afraid on a runaway horse. Some people seize up. Some people turn cold and clear inside, like Clay, and only start to shake afterward. Annie sails into trouble like she wants it to last forever, like she can skim off from fear only what's precious. She almost never comes off.

Try acting like you're the boss, Clay says when they circle past him.

Annie will never reach the level where she can ride for money if she can't get over this taste for fun. Last month at a three-day event up in Dixon, she let Pablo strut his stuff in the dressage test on the first day, with the cross-country course and the show jumping still ahead of her. The judges disqualified her for putting the other riders at risk. When she led Pablo out of the ring, people came over to tell her what a shame it was, and she turned to Clay and said, They don't get it.

Pablo starts sidestepping in the corner, getting ready to shoot out from under her again, and Annie doesn't even bother to try to stay a step ahead of him.

Clay hollers at her. I want to marry you now that you're rich. What do you say? Yes or no?

Pablo rears, and like a fool, Annie falls forward on his neck when he comes down, sending him into a real panic. He surges to a gallop, and Annie locks her fingers in his mane to keep from being thrown. Clumsily she recovers, shoving her feet back in the stirrups and sawing on the reins. Clay just about falls off the fence laughing.

Annie fights Pablo to a halt. I'll get you for that, she says.

Leading her horse back to the barn, Sharon keeps asking Clay if the horse is good enough. She's been taking lessons for a year, long enough, by her lights, to run out and buy a twenty-thousand-dollar gelding that Clay has to ride for her until she learns what to do with him.

Sure, Clay says. Good enough.

In the late-afternoon light Sharon's blond hair gleams. Hair he wants to touch even though he knows it will feel brittle when he does.

She matches her step to the horse's, just as Clay does, an unconscious adjustment. Clay must have been seven the first time he bridled a horse for himself. He did what he'd watched his father do: without unhooking the halter, he looped the lead rope over the horse's neck so he could pull its head down, cup a hand over its nose, and slip the bit between its teeth, but before Clay could tug the bridle over its ears, the horse jerked its head up, lifting him off his feet. He didn't try to get even by yanking on the rope—it would be stupid to be brutal to a creature that never had to submit to you. All you could really do was sidle within the shadow of its power.

Sharon says, I can see what you're telling me about getting him on the bit, but I don't know how to do it when I'm the one up on his back.

You can't really get it from being told how, Clay says. You have to memorize what you're doing with your body when it's going right.

She hangs on his every word. He imagines that once she leaves the property, she's able to take a certain view of him, but here he's a movie star and the Dalai Lama rolled into one.

I'm just not used to being a novice, Sharon says. Whenever I think I'm doing it right, I'm not.

Yeah. Clay has banged away at his guitar enough times, fumbling for the next chord. Not exactly music.

Let me take care of that, Clay says. I like telling you when you're wrong.

Sharon slaps Clay's arm with the reins. I've noticed.

All the women flirt with him. Not just the worshipful teen-agers in his lessons but grown women with husbands and children. Clay doesn't get many actual offers, but there's always an imminent possibility. Just as it's always possible he and Annie might take another tumble. Around the horses all his pores are open to even the slightest physical cues, and even the slightest cue demands a blunt reaction, every gesture enlarged, coarser, harder, out of the need to hold your own against a creature who outweighs you by over a thousand pounds. Annie used to tease him about his harem, but she doesn't care. She has always been open-handed with him, from that first time, when she cut him off and got out of his bed and went about her business.

Clay enters the barn through the doorway on the left. The barn is split down the middle, two corridors flanked by stalls, connected only by a narrow passageway that bisects the barn. On the left, they house the horses that belong to people who can afford box stalls, mostly the folks who train with Ryan Callahan, the big-time trainer who keeps the barn afloat. On the right, they keep the workaday horses they use for lessons and the rest of the boarders' horses. Sharon has a box stall.

In the tacking area Clay exchanges Carillon's bridle for a halter and clips him to the ties. He tells Sharon to brush the horse while he stows her saddle and bridle. On his way out of the tack room, he bumps into Annie, lugging another saddle. He heaves it onto a rack for her, and when he turns around, Ryan Callahan is standing in the doorway, with the genial look on his face that means he's about to ask them to do something they were already supposed to have done.

Hey, Ryan says. I have a training session at five, and it looks like no one's dragged the arena yet.

They keep a small tractor, no bigger than a forklift, for raking the sandy soil in the riding arena to make the footing more secure. In the tack room Ryan posts a weekly calendar that charts the times he'll need the arena. He has first dibs on it. The stable hands are supposed to rake it just before he uses it, but they don't speak English and they can't read the calendar.

That should be Esai who does that, Clay says.

Thanks, Annie says. Thanks for letting us know.

The man hasn't come to do them any favors, but Annie's a schoolgirl about Ryan Callahan too. Clay sometimes catches her leaning on the arena rail with the girls who take lessons from her, watching in silent awe as one of Ryan's people takes jumps or Ryan schools one of his clients' horses. Callahan has them soak his horses' hay before feeding them, because he has some theory that breathing in the dust and fine seeds in the hay is bad for his horses' lungs, and now Annie soaks Pablo's hay before she gives it to him. In his box stall, which she snatched for him when a boarder left, as if it were his due.

Ryan checks his watch. My rider will be here in ten minutes.

We'll see what we can do for you, Clay says.

As far as Clay is concerned, raking the arena is a little extra that isn't strictly owed. They don't do it on demand for anyone else. Ryan's clients don't even tack up their own horses but wait for the stable hands to deliver them. To these people, the horses are just expensive equipment. If Clay makes sure the horses are fed and watered and housed in clean stalls, keeps track of who's lame and who's sound and who needs the vet and who needs a farrier, balances the books for one more month, then he can get away with everything else.

I don't like to have to ask every time, Ryan says, in such an apologetic way that Clay can't be sure he's making a complaint.

I'll rake the arena, Annie says. I'll do it right now.

Ryan smiles at her. Thanks, sweetie. I knew I could count on you.

That's not your job, Clay says.

Annie puts her hand out. Give me the keys to the tractor.

She smells like liniment and horse sweat. Every day she

slathers DMSO on Pablo's swollen leg. The salve stinks like garlic, and they wear gloves when they apply it, to keep it from getting on their skin. And still the odor clings to Annie's clothes.

Clay shrugs. He says, Esai has the keys.

He leaves Annie to apologize some more and promise she'll track down Esai right away. She has started snooping in Clay's bills to see if he can afford to pay her, and now she lectures him about the size of the vet bill, which he's had to carry from month to month. Two thousand dollars. Her first big check from grandma will be coming in soon. Instead of paying her, he should ask her for a loan.

Clay finds Sharon kissing her horse's nose, and she blushes like a kid. Clay does not mind the kind of rich person Sharon is. The kind who hang around the barn cleaning tack and blithely trash their Volvos with their muddy riding gear. He doesn't care about money either.

They work on opposite sides of the horse to groom him. Just circling the brushes requires an expanded range of motion, fully extended arms.

Damn, Sharon says. I broke a nail.

Clay rests his elbows on the horse's back. I thought you wanted me to take you seriously.

I don't care, she says. I *wouldn't* care, except Bill and I have a dinner date, and I'll have to rush home to get out of these jeans and into pantyhose, and now I'll have to repair the damn nail. If I keep him waiting, he'll complain about how much time I spend here.

The husband has never joined Sharon at the barn, though he must bankroll her hobby.

What a lot of work you must have with him, Clay says.

Sharon tosses the brush at him, and Carillon jerks in the ties. She doesn't bother to soothe the horse.

Clay retrieves the brush and slaps it into Sharon's palm. She doesn't close her fist. She leans in close and runs her hand down his arm. Light sparks off the bangles that slither on her wrist.

And then Annie comes scuffing along in her unlaced riding boots, her cupped hands pressed against her chest. She starts at the sight of them, and Sharon takes a step back from Clay. Annie's not jealous. She'll holler at him later, tell him only barn animals do it out in the open.

Annie says, I can't find Esai and I can't find the keys.

Then I guess you can't drag the arena, Clay says.

Is this some kind of pissing contest with Ryan?

She shouldn't speak to him like this in front of Sharon. Sharon might put two and two together and figure out Annie is something more than hired help. This skinny rail of a kid with her hands clutched over her heart.

Annie ducks under the ties to stand smack in front of him. Do you *want* him to find another barn?

Why would she imagine Ryan Callahan would move his entire stable of horses over some puny little oversight? Clay has a moment when he almost feels sorry for her, concocting another drama in which everything is on the line. She told him once how she broke with her parents. She couldn't just let them know she wanted to take a year or two off school. No, she had to have a screaming fight and finish it by punching a window. She has scars between her knuckles, jagged lines stippled with bumps, as if shards of glass are still embedded beneath the skin.

Clay laughs. People let you get away with the little stuff.

Annie snaps her hands open with the flourish of a magician, and out pops a garter snake, an S-curve lashing the air. Clay screams and jumps back, Sharon shrieks, and the horse whinnies and jerks its haunches to the side. The snake skims across the floor, sickening smooth ripple of muscle.

They have rules. No pranks involving tack. No collateral damage to third parties.

Damn it, Annie, Clay says. Not around the horses.

It's Annie's turn to laugh. I told you I'd get you back.

Clay sits in a chair, his head tilted back on the lip of the laundry sink, while Annie runs the water till it's warm. In his lap he cradles his arm in its clean white cast. It's her fault, so she has to wash his hair. She had come to sit beside him on the fence while he taught a group lesson. When the kid on Sunny lost control of the mare and started careening around the arena, Clay hollered at the other riders to halt and dismount. He knew by the look on the kid's face that she would come off, and he felt the familiar dread of waiting for what had to happen. Then Annie jumped off the rail and ran into the path of the mare, waving her arms. Sunny half-reared, and Annie jumped to catch the reins and got dragged off her feet. Stupid! And it was his lesson, so he had to go out there and tackle the damn horse before it trampled her. At first he thought he could get by splinting the broken arm himself; the wraps they used on the horses' legs were just as good as Ace bandages, and he could make a splint from a dowel. But the splint kept slipping and finally he went to the emergency room for a cast. It was worth it, to get the Vicodin. It always makes him feel happy and horny.

Annie wets his hair with the spray attachment on the

faucet. Instead of leaning over to give him a shampoo, the way a hairdresser would, she straddles his lap, standing with one leg on either side of his. He closes his eyes and lets his head bob under her fingers.

Her talk is as lulling as the motion of her hands. She's got a five-year plan for herself and Pablo. If she trains hard, they'll be ready for national competitions in about two years.

Clay has helped her trailer Pablo to a couple of local three-day events. She gets so nervous she pukes before she rides. The judging is at best unreliable, and she can't make up her mind if it would be an insult to win a ribbon, or worth the trouble of spoiling Pablo's fun. In her pipe dreams she never imagines she'll be measured on any terms but her own, and she has never even asked him if he thought she had the kind of talent—huge talent—it took to compete nationally.

Her thighs feel warm against his, even through his jeans. She's wearing the clothes she sleeps in, a tank top and thin cotton sweatpants, and the soft nubs of her small breasts tap against his chest in rhythm with the motion of her hands.

That's got to be enough shampooing, he says.

I'm giving you a scalp massage, you ingrate, Annie says.

She gets up to rinse his hair, and he leans forward to reach for the towel.

She yanks his head back. I have to put in conditioner.

Annie straddles his lap again to apply the conditioner, and her hair falls forward. He could take a strand of it into his mouth if he wanted to. Black, black hair that she almost never wears loose like this. She thumbs his scalp, hard, the muscles that wrap her shoulders and brace her collarbone tensing and releasing as she works.

How come you never did? she says.

Never did what?

Compete seriously, she says. You can ride.

He grew up riding Western on his father's farm, which comes in handy whenever he breaks an arm and has to ride one-handed. Horses were for work or for riding hell-bent for leather in the foothills near the farm. Not for prancing around arenas. Stupid little stuff mattered too much in competition—oiling your boots till they gleamed, tipping your hat to the judges before you began.

I don't like prissy rich people, he says.

Remind me to tell that to Sharon, Annie says.

Clay smiles. She's not prissy.

Then what about Jerry?

Jerry's money pays for the barn, but theoretically Clay gets a 20 percent share in exchange for his work.

He's just a silent partner, Clay says. I do the chores so he doesn't get bothered, and he signs the checks so I don't get bothered. That's what you call a good working arrangement. It's not the same thing as needing some fat cat to sponsor you on a good horse.

Why not? You still have to worry about pissing him off.

Clay shrugs.

He doesn't worry about it. He learned from his father a useful economy of effort. To save money, his father didn't wire their barn for electricity but used a kerosene lamp that would have sent the place up in flames if it tipped over. When Clay was just a boy, he was allowed to light the wick and carry the lamp and hang it from a hook high above his head. When his father caught Clay's eyes skidding toward that lamp, the liquid alight within it, he schooled Clay to set it down carefully and forget about it.

Annie circles her thumbs at his temples. You bought that new horse without even asking him, when you still haven't paid the vet.

There's this side of her that loves to scold. If she finds him behind the barn smoking a joint, she takes it out of his mouth and lectures: Not before a lesson.

You are so uptight, he says. Why don't you take some of my Vicodin?

You have a primitive philosophy.

What would you know about philosophy? You spend all your free time watching reality TV.

She tugs on his hair. Asshole, she says.

Just about every night she watches whatever kind of reality show there is, unless she's replaying her videos of the international three-day event championships, over and over. She never reads any of the college textbooks on the shelf in her bedroom. Whenever they end up sleeping together in her bed, he looks at those books and thinks she is bound to get bored of this prolonged temper tantrum. But he hasn't been in her bed for a while, or she in his. He can't decide which of them hasn't been interested.

Annie moves to the sink to rinse his hair. Ryan said he could give me a few pointers. It wouldn't take anything away from training with you.

Maybe this is why she was so eager to drag the arena for Ryan last week.

That guy can be of use to you, Clay says.

He reaches for the towel again, but Annie grabs it first and settles back in his lap to dry his hair.

You have beautiful hair, she says.

Now her hips and her shoulders move in tandem with her working hands. His arm throbs in its cast, and there's another throbbing in his gut that means he's about to get an erection. She's playing him. But two can play this game.

He sneaks an arm around her waist. She gives him a look he's seen before. When Sunny banged him against the railing and snapped his arm, pitching Clay on the ground, Annie stood over him, feet planted, her fingers snarled in the mare's reins, dust smeared on her face, caked on her clothes. She studied him in a way that erased familiarity, as if she were double-checking the math of his trajectory and its unimpressive result. She could have been the one who got knocked on her ass. The horse dragged her a good thirty feet.

He lifts the hem of her tank top to expose a swatch of purpled skin. Sunny bruised you pretty bad.

She pushes her shirt down. What are you bothering me for? I thought you were getting that from Sharon.

Even though the sun has not quite set and it's against one of Annie's rules for herself to drink before dark, she and Clay are drinking beer on the porch. Someone is still working a horse in the arena, sending up clouds of dust that drift over to them, making Clay cough. But it's too hot to sit inside.

Annie rubs her eyes. If he has a bowed tendon, she says.

Pablo came up lame again today after Annie's training session with Clay. They have spent the last hour cold hosing the horse and treating his leg.

Annie's eyes water, but she could have gotten some of that stinging salve on her hands. Clay has never seen her cry, except maybe once. It was too dark to be sure, which was the point of riding the trails together at night, another kind of lesson he was giving her. They knew what they couldn't see—the steep slopes where one misstep would send horse and rider tumbling, the patches of trail studded by rocks, the passages where sharp branches of live oak whipped your face if you failed to duck—and they had to discipline themselves not to telegraph anticipation to the horses but let them pick their way, teeter between knowing what was ahead and refusing to know, rhythm you got just right or not at all. That night she had to get ahead of him, showing off, and she didn't give him a chance to tell her a tree had come down across the trail. He pulled up and she didn't, and she came off. When he hauled her to her feet, she said, You knew it was there, and he told her not to whine and she slugged him. Maybe she was crying.

If he has a bowed tendon, Annie says, he'll never be able to do anything but flat work. I won't be able to event with him.

She didn't just let Pablo have his head today. Clay watched her, no longer listening with her body, sitting the canter like a slob, fisting her hands on the reins instead of keeping them open, begging the horse to go berserk on her. Clay has never lied to her—no surprise, his flirting with Sharon, and he's promised she won't catch them at it if it goes any further—but he doesn't need to hammer her with the truth.

He says, Don't let him pull any of that bucking bronco stuff.

That's up to Pablo.

You want him sound, don't you?

You don't get it, she says.

If she loves the goddamn horse so much, then she should have thought about the consequences when she rode him today. Trying to make it happen.

You're not stuck, he says. You can afford to keep him as a pet and buy another horse.

Like this is about the money.

Isn't it? That trust money has yanked the rug right out from under you.

This ought to get her going, but she only says, I feel sorry for you.

As if her way of fucking up is any different to his.

He's so mad he has to get up and leave. He heads for the barn because he has nowhere else to go to escape her unless he jumps into his truck. He's angry at himself for getting angry. Let her find out for herself that crashing into things will land her in the same place it lands everyone else. Even if she manages to split her skull open, she won't be seeing any stars.

He decides to clean tack. That always makes him feel right with the world.

He has just pulled down a couple of tangled bridles to work on when Sharon comes to the door of the tack room.

Hey, he says. I didn't know you were still here.

She'd stopped to chat when he and Annie were hosing Pablo's leg, and he never checked to see if her car was still in the parking lot. He has promised Annie only to be discreet. She's not likely to come looking for him at the moment.

Sharon shuts the door behind her, and when she's close enough to kiss, he backs her against the wall, using his cast like a club, leveraging this advantage, and presses his mouth to hers. They rake each other's mouths with their tongues, no effort wasted on preliminaries. They'll take what they can, right now, calibrating exactly how fast the end will rush at them.

She wrenches her mouth from his. I have to go, she says. We have tickets to the opera tonight and it's over an hour's drive.

He pins her arm and nuzzles her neck so he can try to leave a bruise there, a small bruise for Bill or Ben or whatever-his-name-is to fail to notice. There's not a chance in hell that Sharon will let Clay make her late to her opera.

But still she has to plead with him, bracing an arm against his chest. Maybe—maybe Thursday we can take your truck somewhere.

I'll walk you to your car, he says.

When they come out of the barn, dusk is turning to darkness. Annie has turned on the porch light, and Clay can see her silhouetted against the wall, leaning back in her chair, the beer bottle still in her hand. He doesn't know if she can see him, hip to hip with Sharon. When they arrive at her car, he waits till Sharon opens the door and the interior light comes on before he leans in for one last kiss.

He doesn't turn to face the house until Sharon pulls out of the parking lot. He expects Annie to leap at him from the porch and douse him with her beer. She has had time to plan her revenge, and he has it coming, because he promised to clean up his act.

But she stays seated. She watches him come toward her, and he can't avert his eyes. She sets the beer bottle down, and it tips and spills and he can hear the foam hissing and she doesn't right it.

She puts her head down on the table.

This is no submission. A girl like her will never stay here with him in a house looking out over a parking lot and a dusty riding ring, and she will never admit that she must tote her losses and go. Even from a distance he can tell that she is trembling, something in her willful self amplifying even the smallest vibration. What he has always liked most about making love to her is the right to put his hand on her hard little belly; she is so thin he can feel her blood pulse at her navel, as if a second heart pumped mightily there.

Once he woke up after a night of partying to discover that someone had bleached his eyebrows while he slept. Once he woke up stuffed into an empty sack of feed. He's waking up now, deep in muck. Amazed.

Last of the True Believers

Neil came in the back door whistling. When he shoveled me up in his arms, he nearly lifted me from the chair where I was slumped over a cup of coffee.

By proxy he prodded me from bed every morning, my clock radio set to go off in time to catch the last few minutes of his talk show. Before I even woke up, he had put in several hours at work, been out and about long enough to come across some-one or something he needed to tell me about.

After he nuzzled me, he said, Those idiots still haven't towed that abandoned car.

The car had been there a month, parked in front of our house, missing its radio, its tires collapsed on their metal wheel rims.

I wasn't really ready yet for the spit and crackle of his outrage, cheery or not. I never was, and he never noticed, a pact we had honored for so long it would hold even if the ground gave way beneath us.

I said, Then you better go and bother *them*.

It's no use calling the city, he said. All you get is voice mail. If somebody left that car in the hills, it would be whisked away in record time.

On the hills to the east of us, the houses of the rich climbed in literal aspiration. In our neighborhood in the Berkeley flats we had to hound the city about sidewalk repair and dumped cars, clear our kids out of the local park by dusk, and scan the ground the next morning for used condoms. Not a poor neighborhood, though a few blocks south of us people had to worry about drug dealers setting up shop, and if some houses had unkempt yards or boarded-up windows, others were fiercely, proudly tidy.

That's what the bureaucracy counts on, Neil said. That working people will always be too tired. Maybe I can browbeat the neighbors into signing a petition.

Couldn't you just file a complaint online? I said.

Neil gave me a smacking kiss.

Things had settled down, but I still enjoyed chafing at his need for everything to be mutual, and apparently he got a kick out of it too. Nothing major, just little spats over how to handle the kids or whether I needed to sneak off for a massage at a spa with soothing flute music when Neil had a perfectly good pair of hands. I used to be scared by the thought of bickering, that miserable married fate, but resistance had turned out so surprisingly to make me feel gleeful. Lighter.

When Neil closed in again, I pushed him off. I said I had to get the girls up for school.

He wasn't usually here for that. After he finished his three-hour shift, he liked to stop at a diner on his way home. Even on weekends Neil got up at five and stole out the door to get a cup of coffee someplace where the crockery was thick and chipped, the waitresses wore aprons, and the regulars took a stool at the counter. He talked to anyone who sat down next to him. He'd gotten the job at the station because one morning at the counter he improvised a rant about bumper stickers for a woman who turned out to be the program director. In a few weeks he'd mastered how to run the electronic board that spliced in commercials, prerecorded messages, and phone calls for his program.

Neil wasn't put off by my shove. He lifted my hair and kissed the back of my neck. You're so beautiful, he said. I love you so much.

This sweet, belated, alarming inrush of passion, after nearly sixteen years together and three kids. For sure we were through it, in the ebb of it now.

I was kissing him back when Molly walked in on us.

Take that somewhere else! she said.

Whenever she caught us kissing or holding hands or slapping ass, Molly pitched a fit, and she nearly always caught us, because as soon as she hit puberty she'd acquired a nose for it, a vigilant sense of our trespass on turf that ought to be hers. She'd just turned fourteen, so you could say this was merely in the course of things, her excruciating sense of privacy. She had to pin her arms to her sides and duck her head whenever her father—suddenly *a man*—gave her a hug. She had to set her own alarm in the morning to keep us from leaning over her in her bed. She had to lock herself in the bathroom to do makeup and her hair, muffle even her crying when she couldn't get it right.

She brushed past us to root in the cupboard for a box of cereal. She was still wearing the sweatpants and T-shirt she'd slept in—no more flimsy nightgowns—so I couldn't tell if she'd put on her leg brace, which she was supposed to do as soon as she got out of bed.

Molly smacked a bowl and the cereal box on the table and sat across from me. She said to her father, I caught the end of your show. Are you trying to lose your job?

Whoa, Neil said. I missed something here.

It used to be just teasing, Neil playing along with a general female clucking over his male ineptitude: resident clumsy oaf, a little obtuse, a little obstinate. There was something serious, separate now, in Molly's condescension. Whenever I tried to talk to Neil about it—how much of this is just growing up?—he said, She's no different from any of her friends.

With her fingernail Molly scraped at a chip in the Formica tabletop. The table had never been better than beat-up, but its surface was beginning to look scabbed over. She'd picked up the habit when she was cooped up at home, recovering.

Explain yourself, mister, she said. I'm waiting.

She'd acquired the brace at about the same time she began to grow breasts and hips. When we got the call last August, Neil and I raced to the emergency room expecting she'd need a cast or stitches. We found her lying on a gurney, already prepped for surgery, doped up, hazy-eyed. When she saw us, she said, Mommy! Daddy!

We'd been told she'd fallen off her bike. Once we got to her, she would be all right. Primitive and simple, that belief, and so devious the ways in which Neil and I would try to recover our headlong rush, go to war with the facts and with each other. She'd hit a retaining wall, flown through the air still on the bike, spiking the pedal through her leg when she landed. She'd gashed an artery below the knee. The leg would atrophy. She'd always need a brace.

What gives you the idea I'm going to lose my job? Neil said.

Molly wagged a finger at him. You're not supposed to talk about the new management on the air. You said they warned you twice.

I caught that last bit too. The station had been a Berkeley-leftie backwater for so many years—Neil could say anything on the air—and they were all a little provoked at having to contemplate market share and an aging demographic. But Neil had made an end run around the ban on criticizing the new regime. He claimed they'd instituted a dress code—no more bandannas and frayed jeans—and invited listeners to call in and let him know if they could tell he was wearing a tie this morning. Neil hadn't worn a tie since his high-school graduation.

Don't worry, he said. I know what I can get away with.

There *is* a principle in there somewhere, I said.

I can't believe you're taking his side, Molly said. Like it's all just a prank, and nobody gets hurt.

Neil grinned. I promise not to put you girls out on the streets to beg.

That reminds me, I said. We'll be late for school if I don't get your sisters up.

Molly rolled her eyes. You should both lose your license to parent.

I was happy to head down the hall to fetch Carrie and Emma. Sometimes we pretended we couldn't tell them apart, two towheads, nearly the same size, best pals: Now which one of you little ones is seven, and which one of you is eight? I thought they liked it. I knew they liked me to stroke their cheeks, kiss them awake, swaddle them in their covers for a hug. I still had plenty more coming from them. But Molly was all right. No kid could hop out of bed so snarky unless she was full of love for herself, healthy. And she wasn't really worried her father would lose his job. We joked about that too. How he'd end up on Telegraph Avenue, on the sidewalks near the university where jammed in among the tables of street vendors selling tie-dyed shirts and tarnished silver jewelry were the tables of political crusaders, littered with leaflets. Sometimes you passed a table where a tape recorder instead of a person harangued you.

And if he got canned—he'd been at this job four years, a long time for him. It was only thirty hours a week, counting prep time, which he could do whenever, and Neil always knew how to fill the gaps, pick up a few extra bucks as a handyman or a temporary research assistant for someone at UC-Berkeley. He'd worked on a linguistics study once, every bit as interesting as what he garnered from the delivery truck drivers and street people and physics professors he came across at the diner. We'd be all right without the money so long as we could keep our old Toyota truck running and I could haul my gardening tools to customers' houses. Neil could patch that engine with Scotch tape and spit.

So enticing now to dwell on things I minded, and I minded losing the health insurance. Which new management had extended to part-timers at the station, and I didn't care if their motives ought to be mistrusted and the gesture came too late to cover Molly's bills from last year.

I left another man for Neil. A math professor, whom I'd followed to a little college town in western Massachusetts where the only work I could find was writing questions for a college testing service. And then my old college friend Neil showed up, on his way around the country. In that place where I could find nothing to do, Neil went out early in the morning and came back to tell me how he'd helped a neighbor hoist a blue milk crate into a tree in the hope of attracting an owl to nest there, promised to take me out later to a spot where he'd discovered a covey of quail, showed me rubbings he'd made from tombstones in the local cemetery, grainy renderings of beautiful serif letters hammered singly and unevenly into stone, bas-relief angels holding trumpets aloft, chiseled crucifixes. We'd both grown up working class, been the first members of our families to go to college, felt the pressure to make it up and out. But Neil was thinking he might winter in California, where it would be easy to live out of his truck. He wanted to know if I'd like to come. I said yes.

We lived in that truck for a couple years. Once we got to San Francisco, we parked every night at China Basin. We knew which diners had all-you-can-eat specials, where to take a shower (pay seventy-five cents at the city pools), how to qualify for treatment at a free medical clinic. If it got too cold at night, I slept with socks pulled over my hands. So I could thaw out in the morning, Neil learned how to start a smokeless fire in a metal garbage can, tamped so that a cop driving by wouldn't stop to investigate. When I got pregnant, Neil was the one who said we couldn't live in a truck with a baby. We found a place we could afford in Berkeley, where rent control was decent.

Neil liked to say, work the system. We had finessed our cash income so we could get Medi-Cal for the kids. When Molly had to have a second surgery, Neil got her in to see a specialist at Stanford. All of them wrote off a certain amount of their practice. And then he did his homework and found that the county hospital had excellent physical therapy, you just had to wait when you arrived for an appointment, and I learned how to put her through exercises to slow the attrition of wasted muscle. Neil filed the paperwork to homeschool Molly for a few months, and after he came back from the station he spent the morning teaching her English and algebra and Civil War history. Plenty of books in our house for her lessons; if you combed flea markets and garage sales, you could land some terrific finds. Molly kept up with her class and was back in school within three months.

We got her the best care. We were used to the effort of working the system. The satisfaction of it.

When I opened the door to Carrie and Emma's bedroom, I had to stand there a moment until my eyes adjusted to the darkness, wait for the bundle in each bed to be articulated from shadow. Until I was sure I could see them, safe, sound, my heart bubbled for a few beats, faint percussion I hadn't listened for before. This happened to me in the night too: I woke in a silent house and strained, listening for something.

Every Tuesday morning I hauled my gardening tools to the elementary school instead of a client's house. Neil came with me to school: while I worked in the garden with the second and third graders, he did science experiments with Molly's eighth-grade class. I was always happy working in the garden, but really, really happy working with kids their age, bent on competence in the most unself-conscious, unself-critical way: a body just a tool of fraternally equal capability, a pleasure because of what it could be used for, not otherwise worth a fuss. I'd planted flowers with the kids at first, but they were more interested in plants they could eat. We had rows of kale, lettuce, collard greens, beans, carrots, even strawberries, and a bed of native plants—California buckeye, soaproot, Douglas iris, hummingbird sage—whose spring flowering attracted insects birds needed to eat. Gardening with Carrie's and Emma's classes meant I could spend extra time with my own daughters. Molly had needed such intent attention for so many months—her pain a constant urgent summons we couldn't answer—that it was as if Carrie and Emma had gone soft at the edges for me, vague. Who sat next to them at lunch? Which of them wanted hot milk before bed, which was pining for a new watch?

Carrie worked at my elbow scattering mulch, composted from cafeteria food scraps. I gave her a trowel to work the mulch into the soil and knelt to do the same work with my hands. Easier to tell by feel the consistency of soil, to sift it for the veined lacework of desiccated leaves, the papery remains of insects, the velvety tissue of rotting petals.

I had to nudge Carrie to get her to give up her turn with the trowel. We had only four, shared among thirty kids. I supplied all the tools and the PTA held bake sales so we could buy plants and seed. We didn't have any parents who could dig into their own pockets to fund enrichment programs, only a general gung-ho attitude about the grand enterprise of public education.

Carrie found a caterpillar in the dirt and held it in her palm, swiveling her hand so that as it crawled it could keep going over and around, over and around. The other kids came to see, to debate what to do with it. They hated yielding any share of the crop to insects, and every week we had to go over the reasons why we might pay this tithe: So there would be butterflies to pollinate the flowers. Because birds couldn't form eggshells if they didn't get enough protein in the springtime. Because if we just let the aphids be, they'd attract the ladybugs that fed on them. Because if you squished a caterpillar, it would squirt poison juice on you and you'd *die*.

I took any reasons the kids gave for leaving the bugs alone. I'd begun to resent the idea of making lessons out of our time in the garden, constraining them to some stingy notion of utility. I didn't want to explain away their amazement when we dug up ferny carrot plants to discover the plump root. I liked telling them things they wanted to know for their own purposes. (Which part of the pea pod can you eat? Does a worm have eyes?) I liked surprising them with the way that each living thing was connected to every other in this miniature web of being we'd made.

Carrie had cupped her free hand protectively over the caterpillar, and she wanted me to help her find a hiding place.

I don't want a bird to eat it, she said.

A child couldn't be expected to see how her wishes could be snarled in so fragile a weave.

OK, I said. I helped her pick out a plant to set the caterpillar under and make a little tent of leaves and twigs for it and press pebbles in the mud to mark off a perimeter. By the time the teacher came out to call the kids back to class, Carrie was sure her caterpillar would be safe.

I owed her. All that time I'd spent in waiting rooms, where Molly never wanted to talk. Somehow too hard to crack a book when you might be called in two minutes or twenty. There were always the same magazines, *People, Us, Sports Illustrated, Architectural Digest, Better Homes and Gardens*. I got used to a regular fix of interior decoration, kitchens with bleached maple cabinets and sleek living rooms with floor-to-ceiling windows. We had to go back seven times to get her brace refitted so it wouldn't chafe her leg. They're never going to get it right, she said, and I—what did it mean to get it *right*, the blister from two weeks before sunk like a coin in her skin, rimmed by blackened tissue—and I, Neil and I together, had to *hold optimism* for her, the job the hospital social worker had given us. I said, I know they will.

They did get it right that time. And then she grew an inch and we had to go back to get the brace sized up.

Neil was waiting for me in the truck, and he hopped out to help me load the tools. He reported on his session with Molly's class, pleased and a little surprised; they'd contrived batteries that ran on the stored energy in a potato, and it had worked.

It was such an odd expression. Hold optimism. Neil had looked at the woman funny when she told us. Oxygen? he said. You want us to hold oxygen? We still laughed about it, and it was also, Jesus, true, another one of our jobs: not to suck the oxygen out of Molly's air. She'd been at soccer camp last summer and we didn't know what we'd find instead this year and then she showed us a calendar with babysitting jobs already penciled in for June and July. She wanted to know what she should charge.

Neil drove home. He didn't like being a passenger. The stick shift groaned as he worked it patiently, and he promised to have a look at it this weekend.

I should really take a couple days and fix that bad wiring in the kitchen too, he said.

If we used the toaster and the coffeemaker at the same time, we blew a fuse. Neil had been meaning to rewire the outlets.

They're talking about layoffs at the radio station, he said. Smart move. Get you to think twice before you buck in the traces.

Tell me you didn't take the bait.

I confess. I already gave in to temptation this morning.

I thought back to waking up and hearing Neil's voice on the radio, but I couldn't remember anything that would have gotten him in hot water. I couldn't remember anything except health insurance, health insurance, health insurance.

I'm sick of all their daily fucking directives, Neil said. On air you have to refer to President Bush, never just Bush, out of respect for the office. What kind of crap is that?

All of a sudden I didn't want to listen to him work himself into a lather. *I don't want to* such an allurement I almost said the words out loud.

I'm tired, I said. I could use a break from scrambling to pay the bills.

He banged the steering wheel. Don't go making a calamity of it. Things. Work. Out.

Against his principles to hang on to a grudge, lie around steeped in regret. If I complained about our rusted-out washing machine, he'd just disembowel it and put it back together. I hated that he could trip me up on whatever it was I wanted—selfish—just by being able to adapt and scavenge and keep moving.

He didn't know that. He was already reaching for my hand.

I can always go back to organizing, he said. The timing is right. Americans are kind of like locusts—seventeen years of dormancy and then they swarm. We're back to war protests. Everyone's finally taking to heart the dire predictions about the polar ice caps melting. Do something!

If I brought up health insurance, he'd give me such a look. I'd expected Neil to disapprove when I set up the gardening business, because after all, who were these people who paid others to weed their yards and prune their bushes? But he didn't. He went to the library and researched the cultivation of native plants, drought tolerant and not water hungry, and connected me to a botanist up in Point Reyes who really knew what she was doing, and now I pushed native landscaping on all my clients. I wasn't just a laborer like my father, who did yard work as a second job in summer, once in a while getting a glass of ice water at the back door. My clients took notes on what I told them.

Neil parked in our driveway and plucked the keys from the ignition.

He said, Oh shit, when he saw the abandoned car still in front of our house. After he'd collected signatures from our neighbors, who may or may not have resented his noblesse oblige, and delivered the petition in person to our city councilwoman's office, he'd extracted a promise from an aide that something would be done. Someone had come and put a Denver boot on one of the punctured tires.

Those folks at city hall have a wicked sense of humor, I said.

He should have handed me the keys so I could go on to work. But he said, Come in for coffee.

I had two yards to do that afternoon, but I said yes.

We skipped the coffee and went to bed. We'd taken to having sex instead of lunch in the middle of the day. For months we hadn't made love—it felt like sneaking off duty when there were so many chores and then the work of divvying them up, who'd take her to which appointment, make the next phone call on the list, get up that night if she called for us. Of course we got pissed at each other, just little skirmishes, as if each of us was trying to tease out the true strength of the other before committing to real battle. We'd clash so briefly, so fiercely, for such inconclusive gains, because who could say for sure if she cried from pain or for no reason—and I'd never forgive Neil that distinction—and who knew if we should correct her just as we always had when she picked a fight with Carrie or Emma? How many ways could you parse loyalty, and loyalty to what? The day I found a couple pairs of Molly's shorts shoved in the garbage, I wanted to go and hold her, and Neil, in a fury, stopped me: Wash them and put them back in her drawer.

The first few times we made love again, I couldn't come. But we found that there was more as well as less to our lovemaking. Neil said we had to be open about it. Be willing to try things we hadn't tried before, till we found our rhythm again. We could touch ourselves in front of each other. Share our fantasies. He wanted to undress me, when for years we'd just shucked our clothes and done it with the lights turned low. He wanted to tell me over and over how beautiful I was. For all of it, I felt embarrassed, doubtful—well, I don't know about that—but harboring secrets turned out to be erotic. What a head of steam we could build up from all the grievances we hadn't aired.

When we made love now I had the sensation that I was falling, unfurling like a ribbon from the fixed, distant point of my body. Tears stung my eyes when he reached orgasm inside me. Tears he didn't acknowledge. Something lush about keeping that to myself too.

On Friday when I came home from work, I stepped into a kitchen that looked as if it had been demolished in my absence. A ragged hole had been hacked into the wall to expose the electrical box, spilling loose wires, coiled and tangled like guts. The air was laden with dust, and chunks of drywall littered the counter and the linoleum floor. Neil did what he pleased to the house. The landlord claimed he couldn't afford repairs, but tenancy law in Berkeley entitled us to subtract supplies and labor from the rent. We'd need to produce a permit to take the deduction, and Neil hadn't had time to get one, though he would do everything exactly to code.

I didn't know if Neil had made a late start or the job had unexpected complications or he'd just been so busy doing as he pleased that he hadn't gotten around to cleaning up so we could throw dinner together. I'd lingered too long at work that afternoon. My last client of the day had come home early and offered me iced tea on her deck. We went out through the French doors off her dining room and sat on a cushioned teak bench in dappled shade, watching water percolate in her stone fountain.

I could hear Neil and Molly in the living room, arguing, and I dropped the grocery bag on the counter, thinking I'd go in there and collar him: put that kitchen back the way you found it.

Carrie and Emma sat on the sofa with their father, curled against him. Molly stood facing Neil, arms crossed, as ready as he was to fight.

What are you going to do there? Neil said. Window-shop. Paw all the crap they put out to lure kids like you onto the wheel of materialist appetite.

Molly said, Let me translate for you, Mom. He won't let me go to the mall with my friends.

Carrie and Emma stared up at Neil, uncomprehending but solemn with the conviction of his authority. Their shirts were smeared with drywall dust, their hair, like his, powdered with it. They must have been helping him. Neil was the perfect father for little girls, ready to join in when they wanted to dismantle the phone to see its parts, confident they could handle the power tools he put in their hands, eager to sweep them up in the free-for-all of his enthusiasms. Stacked around the living room were all the magazines and newspapers he combed daily for radio material, from an ornithology journal to the John Birch Society newsletter. He was dead set on not doing that much longer. Another snipe at management this morning, as if so much rode on the refusal to yield.

And while he was in the mood, Neil meant to give Molly a taste of it too. He said, You don't understand the end purpose of consumer capitalism. To make you feel dissatisfied every waking minute of your life.

Molly wailed, Mom! I just want to go to the mall. I've got stuff to do there. It's *my* babysitting money.

Neil snorted. Which you could use more wisely than to buy some ten-dollar pair of sneakers with eighty dollars' worth of bells and whistles.

I don't want sneakers, Molly said with contempt.

Carrie fidgeted on the sofa, streaking the dark fabric with

putty-colored dust. Not that a few more stains mattered. Molly wouldn't even sit on the sofa anymore. She claimed it smelled funky.

I need jeans, Molly said. I only have three pairs, and none of them fit.

She was wearing flare-leg jeans that probably dated from the seventies, the closest the thrift store could provide to something trendy, and an old sweatshirt of her father's, way too big for her. Snap decision, the either/or choice made by girls her age: midriff-baring T-shirts or these huge sweatshirts that shielded them from the suddenly public and expropriated meaning of their bodies.

Let her go with her friends, I said.

Neil wouldn't look at me. Thanks for the backup.

To Molly he said, At least learn to recognize when you're being manipulated.

Molly gave me a look of practiced exasperation. I wish he'd just get on my case for no good reason, like a normal father.

She had him. And she had me too. The forgotten female conspiracy.

Thank God it's four against one in this house, I said.

Emma slid off the sofa, and Carrie followed her, bound by whatever invisible rope held them together.

Emma came to me and plucked at my sleeve. I don't understand, she said. I don't know what they're saying.

Be glad you're still little, Molly said.

I *am* glad, Emma said. Right, Mom?

Molly ruffled her hair. No need to stalk off. She calmly collected her purse and detoured around her father on the sofa to kiss me good-bye before she headed out the door.

Carrie had already nosed her way under my other arm. I called after Molly, Be back by nine thirty.

From the sofa, Neil said, Weakling.

You could just tell her we can't afford to shop at the mall, I said.

No! Neil said. Then she'd feel deprived.

He just couldn't stop himself. He said, She'll spend her life looking at herself in the mirror and worrying about the hundred ways in which her female body is by definition inadequate.

He had no clue: the pleasure of slipping into new, unmarred clothes, pressed to stiff smoothness, and standing before a full-length mirror, looking over your shoulder at your shape, running your hands over your hips, tucking a collar under, turning out an ankle to see how fabric fell in this pose. Something else that would be missed.

I shook off the girls and went to the kitchen to empty the grocery bags I'd left on the counter. Neil followed me and began unpacking too, a carton of milk, a cereal box, a tub of yogurt.

Why didn't you buy organic milk? he said.

Fuck you, I said.

Neil sighed. OK. I know I stepped in it. But she's all right. She'd take me on again at the drop of a hat, and two more guys twice my size. I won't feel sorry for her.

And he came up behind me and put his arms around me. The dust on his clothes, in his hair, made me sneeze. When he stroked my arms, he left streaks of it on my skin. I was trembling at the way that even rage could be turned for us now.

Neil said, We could try it like this. Filthy.

Why can't you be more open? I said. We go to one of those expensive boutique hotels. With turn-down service. And a

Jacuzzi in the room, big enough for two. And big fat towels that you just throw on the floor after you use them. A room for three hundred dollars a night, minimum.

Neil slept in until six, luxury of the newly unemployed, making half-deliberate noise when he got out of bed and pulled on his pants, belt clanking. When he banged his knee against the bed, I rolled over and yanked the covers tight around me. He sank onto the mattress, burrowed a hand under the blankets to find my back and run his fingers up my spine.

I have an idea, he whispered into my ear, as if this information were seductive.

I didn't say anything.

Let's take off this summer when the girls get out of school, he said. We can rig the truck so we can camp in it, take them across the country if we want to.

Summer is my busy season, I said.

Somebody else can pull weeds for your clients for a few months, he said. Think what it would be like for the girls. Worth a year of school, at least. And we could be scouting out other places to live. Maybe it's time to get away from the city. If we move far enough out in the boondocks, there won't be any malls.

I caught his hand in mine, to make him stop. No, I said.

You can't be mad at me for getting fired.

You would have been laid off anyway.

He'd pushed and pushed as the deadline for layoffs loomed. Why bother? Why go to all that trouble so you wouldn't have to admit dreary defeat? How could I even care, when I knew it was always waiting, the chores, the monotony of thrift, the busy resourcefulness that only meant you'd get up and do it the next day.

Neil slipped his hand free of mine, began circling it along my spine again. He said, Some of the people at the station are talking about staging a walkout.

Great, I said. Maybe you can all go down to Telegraph Avenue and hand out flyers to passersby. Now would be a good time.

He should have let me sleep.

The mattress sagged as Neil pushed himself upright.

You're right, he said. I would have been laid off anyway. They're going to dump a canned program into the dead-loss time slot they used to reserve for kooks like me.

I lay awake for the hour that Neil was gone. When he came back from the diner, he was unapologetically noisy, because I was supposed to be up now.

He snapped the shade on the bedroom window to smack me with the brutal light of day. Staring out the window, he said, That goddamn car is still rotting out there. It's been three months. They think we deserve it here, just like we deserve cracked sidewalks and broken streetlights.

If I couldn't make myself leave the warmth of bed, we'd be late for school.

Did Molly get up? I said.

Yeah, Neil said. She's locked herself in the bathroom, sniffling. She's been in there since I got back.

We'd managed his firing with a show of shrugs for Molly, and she had seemed only a little surprised, a little wistful. But I'd caught her watching me the way I watched her, alert for the least little sign.

In my nightgown I went to wake Carrie and Emma, and then I went to knock on the bathroom door and beg Molly to open it.

She did, just a crack. The makeup she must have applied so carefully was smeared from crying.

I hate these new jeans, she said.

I never wanted to cry when she cried. Maybe before or after but never in sync.

I said, You look fine.

She burst into tears. I look stupid. I spent all my money on them and they're wrong.

She wouldn't let me shop with her anymore, but still I wanted to say, I'll take you back to buy another pair, we'll clean out the store. I had this overwhelming impulse, selfish impulse, to be for once unchecked, to make her another promise that would efface the lewdness of my body under the sheer fabric of my nightgown, the shame of it. So treacherous, this keening to get to her.

You look good, I said. You always look good to me.

She set her face, snapped back into her capable, condescending self. Are we going to be late for school again? she said.

When I came back to pull on some clothes, Neil was still standing at the window, scowling.

Make yourself useful, I said. Carrie and Emma want to bring peanut butter and jelly for lunch.

He backed away from the window, still looking out, before he turned to leave the room. When I shucked my nightgown, I rolled it into a ball and dropped it in the hamper, where it was supposed to go, and then I pulled on jeans and a shapeless, wrinkled T-shirt of Neil's.

I found Neil in the living room with the girls, crowded before the window. Carrie and Emma were not dressed yet, and I doubted he'd thought to start a pot of coffee or pack any lunches.

There's a fire, Carrie breathed.

I leaned over the kids to look out at the abandoned car, rocked gently by the gases of its own combustion, its glass windows shimmering with blue and orange flames that shifted as fluidly as patterns in a kaleidoscope.

Did you call 911? I asked Neil.

Dad, can we go out and watch? Molly asked, but it was only a rhetorical question. She was out the door before her little sisters could even tear off to fetch their clothes.

A siren wailed.

Neil said, Now they'll take it away.

By the time we followed the girls outside, a fire engine blocked the street, and our neighbors were gathering to watch the firefighters hook the hose to a hydrant. Kids were collecting on the sidewalk, elbowing and shoving for a prime spot, and the firefighters hollered at the adults to move them back, the gas tank could explode.

We stood on our neighbor's lawn, most of us with our hands on our kids to keep them still, watching the car burn. The fire in its interior roared, gathering force, and then the windows popped out, spewing pebbles of tempered glass and a wash of heat that pushed us all back from the car.

There were far more firefighters than needed, and some of them joked with us while the others struggled to keep the hose from lashing as water surged through it. When the water hit the flames, they smoked and crackled.

Molly said, It's like the Fourth of July.

One of the firefighters started asking if we'd seen anyone

suspicious on the street this morning. Sometimes street people broke into parked cars to sleep or to smoke, leaving empty bottles on the seat and butts crushed into the mats on the floor.

The way this fire worked, the man said, it looks like it might have been set.

And set carefully, so it would smolder long enough to build up the intense heat required to shatter those windows.

Neil moved through the crowd toward the firefighter. You'll tow this mess away, right?

He'd stood at the window so long, waiting for something.

The firefighter shrugged. That's not our domain.

Neil loomed menacingly over the man. Your domain, their domain. Why can't you just do the right thing? This wreck's been here for months. We've been calling the city, writing, begging on our hands and knees. What does it take to get someone to make it right?

I wanted Neil to shut up, to stop calling attention to himself.

Molly did too. She wove herself beneath Neil's arm.

He's just a regular working stiff, Dad, she said. Might as well let him do his job.

And the man laughed. Yeah, I just punch a clock.

He turned back to the fire, moving slowly, swaying, encumbered by his heavy protective clothing.

I didn't know yet if Neil had done it, only that Molly suspected him too and that her face was alight with satisfaction.

I wish that car would burn for hours, Molly said.

The venom in her voice was as fluid and fierce as fire itself, as the changes it wrought, as the mutability of grief, the thing that shattered and broke, the thing that held you and made you, the thing that turned you to smoke.

She caught her father's arm to keep it around her shoulder, and he looked down at her with an expression she couldn't see. I could.

I would search the garage and if I found oil-soaked rags or a can of gasoline, I'd get rid of the evidence and never tell him. There was so much more that we'd never admit to each other, that only he and I would ever know.

Wait for Instructions

Everything's an emergency to Ethna's mother, but it's Ethna's number she dials, not 911. If only Ethna possessed the full regalia, flashing lights, sirens, a badge, a walkie-talkie hooked to her belt. At least it would reduce the commute to her parents' house at rush hour. She arrives to find her father mowing the lawn, as per her mother's frantic report. He has no business doing this; he's not even allowed to drive yet. The first time Ethna saw him in the hospital, hooked up to tubes, she thought that after all, in spite of his past good health and her mother's years of wearying illness, there might be some justice in the universe. He might be the one packed off to a nursing home, and she might have a few years' peace. Ethna thought, I'm ready. I'm ready!

Her father is walking around with stents in his arteries because her mother warned him not to eat some sausages that had been left in the fridge for weeks. He had to show her, wasteful as she was, wanting to throw out good food. At first they thought it was just food poisoning. He got up to go to work the next morning but couldn't make it out to the car. He puked so hard his new dentures fell into the toilet, and after he mistakenly flushed them, he forbade Ethna's mother to flush the toilet again, because if she ever in her life thought for a moment, she'd know the dentures would clog the sewer pipes. For once Ethna's mother didn't call her for a reality check. For a couple of days the two of them were alone, the toilet filling up with puke and diarrhea and piss and enough bacteria to fell a horse, till her mother called Ethna in tears, saying Eamon couldn't breathe and was refusing to go to the doctor. Ethna had to call an ambulance. After the doctors diagnosed double pneumonia, they got suspicious about all the fluid in his lungs and ran an EKG. Not really the first clue that something was wrong with the man's heart. A week later, her father had a triple bypass.

Even from the curb Ethna can see the effort it takes for her father to push the lawn mower. He's so skinny since his surgery, his skin slack and shriveled, like a tent collapsed on his big frame. But he's slapped on his head the Irish cap he wears for grand occasions, affecting to be what he is, a Kildare farm boy, born and bred. He wants to die in the traces; he's still talking about going back to work despite the doctor's orders to retire.

When Ethna gets out of the car, she stops just out of range of her father's foul breath and motions for him to turn off the mower. He does, but only so he can tackle her, his chest heaving with the effort to take in air. What are you doing here?

His dentures click against his gums, and he winces. He salvaged his old pair to replace the ones he lost, and the poor fit aggravates the coin-sized sores that bloomed in his mouth when he was in the hospital. Some kind of infection. In all their imagining of tortures for him—Ethna, Sean, and Sheila in their teens sharing a joint, piling on the next thing they'd do to their father if they could, hang him upside down, give him the belt for belching at the table—they never came up with anything like what old age could inflict all by itself.

You couldn't get Sean to do this for you, like he promised? Ethna says.

That son of a buck. Claims he's laid up with his back again.

If he were to hear this, Sean wouldn't mind. There's no subtext to her father's concise conversations with her brother: *You knucklehead. Look who's calling who a knucklehead.* Ethna and Sheila shake their heads over Sean, but they both agree it must be harder to be Eamon's son than to be his daughter. Even if he is a little dense, Sean has produced three beautiful kids and hands them over to Ethna every other weekend. With Bobby, Annie, and Ciara, Ethna devises themes for their days together. Oh! I'm *Not* Your Mother! Day means donuts for breakfast, pizza for lunch, and candy for dinner.

Ethna looks at the raggedly stripped lawn and then at her father. I need you to check out my car. The engine's making that ticking noise again.

It's not going to die *click* tomorrow. You get hysterical over nothing.

Click, click. Ethna's vision seems to stutter in time to this perverse punctuation of his. Lately she's been having this problem with blurry vision, but it never lasts for long.

I told you not to go buying some fancy foreign car *click* you can't get parts for, he says. Serves you right. You've *click* got to have the best of everything.

Somehow her confused vision disrupts her other senses, and Ethna hears something muted and mournful in his phlegmy breathing.

Well, she has a more accomplished vocabulary than her brother does. I'm not asking for any favors, she says. If you go listen to the engine for me, I'll finish the lawn for you.

And it's that easy to take care of, and Ethna doesn't even have to look at the house to know her mother hovers at the window, watching anxiously. Ethna finishes the lawn, ignoring her father's complaint that she's not making straight rows—what good are you if you can't do the job properly? When she goes inside to her mother, her father is still tinkering with her car, the engine running and the hood up. His hands, chapped by the cold, scored by a lifetime of banging dented cars back into shape, plunge in and out of the steaming innards of the engine as if something alive is in there and he will throttle it when he gets hold of it.

Ethna halts at the front door, as always, and then forces herself to enter the house. It smells of his sweat.

I knew you'd manage him, her mother says. Will you not stay for dinner?

Sean lives across the bay from San Francisco and can't be expected to make it over here during the week, not with a family of his own, and he's laid up with his back, isn't he? Sheila is in Seattle with her Ph.D. in history and the excuse of her own family too, and there are no more siblings even if there should be, even if the line petered out in a string of miscarriages that ended with the unintended mercy of a doctor cutting out their mother's uterus. And now that Ethna has moved farther away, she can't just pop in and take off. Her mother hates to see her come all that way for nothing.

♦ ♦ ♦ ♦ ♦

Because These Are the Rules:

The Irish have so many children in order to ensure there'll be maiden aunts.

It's the right of the parents to keep one child to care for them in their old age.

The father makes the rules but the mother knits them into your living tissue.

Don't leave. Don't be won over or fooled by the life in this country, the kids in your Catholic grammar school class who chant under their breath, Virgin Virginia Vagina, who aren't struck dumb for blaspheming but join the student council and fill out their college applications and move away and forgo mistrust.

Don't let it show: the hem of your slip beneath your skirt; the boastful kernel that is the product of your American upbringing and that your father will beat out of you if he has to; how afraid you are every time you have to merge into traffic on the highway; the hope you used to feel, every time, that he wouldn't act himself in front of other people, give you the back of his hand or tell your mother to shut her trap; the shame curdling in your belly when they sing, and they always like to sing when they get together, the cousins and aunts and uncles, summoning a tear for Danny boy.

So that you would not marry, the father and mother gave you a name that can be pronounced only by wrinkling the nose and exposing the gums, as if you've just tasted something you'd like to spit out.

Ethna's mother complains in a thready whisper that she can't get his pills into him and she doesn't know what she'll do. Despite the speech therapy Ethna arranged for her, the mild stroke she had last August paralyzed half the muscles in her throat, leaving her unable to speak much above a whisper.

Her ma pleads as if she's before a judge. I'm only trying to help him sort out which pills he's to have when. They're shocking expensive, almost as high as mine. I tell him the doctor says he has to have them, and he just refuses.

Ethna must have been twelve when her mother began confiding in her what her father had done this time. A part of her is still twelve and cannot imagine the rote misery of years behind and years ahead, can only register the present with a perpetually keen impatience.

What's the worst that can happen? Ethna says. If he dies on you, you'll have some peace.

Oh, don't talk like that, her mother says.

Come on, Ethna says. You knew what you were doing when you told him those sausages should be thrown out. That's like waving a red flag before a bull.

Her mother laughs. I have to admit, there's advantages to having him sick. When he was in hospital, I could keep the house nice and toasty.

It *is* cold in here. Ethna doesn't mind their mild winters, and she forgets. She takes her mother by the arm and leads her down the hall to the thermostat. Her father installed it himself a few years ago. The digital display is as effective as the lockbox he used to keep over the old thermostat so her mother wouldn't go wasting his hard-earned money. Ethna gives her mother her hundredth lesson in pressing the keys on the display to adjust the temperature.

Her mother coos amazement. Ethna, master of the material world. She worked her way up from typing reports at the insurance company to managing a database, and she knows better than the programmers how to fool around with the code to make the data accessible. Information can be made to yield its secrets if only you can plumb the order beneath the order. Which turns out to be simple: drop information down a chute where myriad gates send it in either of two directions till it lands in the correct bin. The end user should never have to see or shudder at this cascading sort process, and Ethna's practice in instructing her mother in everyday life has honed her talent for generating a simple interface.

Ethna's Easy-to-Follow Instructions for Irish Old Ladies:

To prevent the microwave from crackling and emitting blue sparks, do not insert dishes covered in aluminum foil.

When the man of the house refuses to write a check for groceries, wait till he is otherwise occupied and go out to his truck in the garage. Insert a grapefruit knife into the lock on the glove compartment and jiggle until the door pops open. Inside you will find a stash of twenties. Remove bills as needed.

When you blow a fuse, do not stand before the fuse box wringing your hands. Consult a daughter if a son is not available. Let her direct you: locate the flipped switch and snap it back to its original position to resume the normal flow of electrical current.

When the doctor prescribes anti-inflammatory drugs for arthritis, hypertension medication, and blood thinners to prevent your next stroke, insisting on non-generic drugs that your insurance company won't cover, do not attempt to solve the problem by halving the daily dose. Have an adult child fax the prescription and a credit-card number to a Canadian discount drug warehouse, allowing time for the pills to arrive in the mail.

When you receive a letter indicating you have won a free weekend at a time-share resort provided you attend an informational meeting at the local Marriott, simply discard the envelope. Do not sign and return the enclosed form, as it is not a necessary courtesy to do so and may incur financial obligation.

Always look a gift horse in the mouth. The next time your husband offers to help you consolidate your credit-card debt, accumulated because your name is not on the checking account, do not accompany him to the bank, where he will instruct the loan officer to garnish 40 percent of your Social Security check to pay off the loan, leaving you not quite enough cash every month to buy the medication he thinks you could do without if you didn't spoil yourself and which he can't pay for with his hard-earned money, not unless he wants to have nothing! nothing! left for his retirement.

Ethna helps her mother start dinner. She dumps chicken into a baking pan, peeling off the skin for the sake of her father's heart, while her mother hastily rinses potatoes and turnips, rock-hard things to be chopped and then boiled till soft. Ethna could have gone home to Lean Cuisine. To distract herself from thoughts of dinner, she delivers a play-by-play of their activity, tossing potato chunks into the pot—and she *scores!*—and telling an invisible interviewer that she owes her improved game to fiber, eating lots of fiber. Her ma nods and smiles vaguely until Ethna backs her against the counter, holding an imaginary mike before her mouth, and demands that she admit she plays to win. Even her ma can't help laughing at her own obedience, at the way the sentence sounds coming out of her mouth, whispery and quivery with Irish vowels: I play to win.

They get around to talking about the grandkids, as they

always do. Sheila is bringing her kids, Nathan and Maeve, for Christmas. They'll stay with Ethna in her new condo, and she'll get to spoil all five of her nieces and nephews. Ethna is already hatching plans for their Gotcha Club, which involves Ethna being able to embarrass the kids in public more often than they can embarrass her (easy to do when you're willing to bust out singing *girls just wanna have fuh-huh-hun* in the line at the movie theater). The kids like having clubs. The Football Club with Bobby, the Light Bulb Joke Exchange with Nathan, the GKA (Girls Kick Ass) Club with Annie and Ciara, who have promised not to tell their parents what the initials stand for and who need someone around who doesn't think girls should be stuck in velvet dresses and shiny shoes. With Maeve, whose mother has made sure she doesn't need any help in this department, Ethna is compiling a list of sayings for the T-shirt company they'll start one day: *It is, like, majorly so. Too bad, so sad. Delightfully tacky, yet refined.*

Ethna peels apples and hands them to her mother so she can hack them and dump them in the pie crust she's made of flour, shortening, and water. Her ma wants advice on Christmas gifts for the kids, and Ethna doesn't bother to steer her toward things she can afford. Not yet. She just listens to her ma's sweet ramblings.

He likes my pies. He shouldn't have pie, really, but God help him, his gout's terrible and now they can't give him anything for it because it's bad for his heart. Where was I? What to get for Annie. She's having a hard time at school, and your brother just leans on her the more. She's lost in the middle between Ciara and Bobby. A middle child has got to peep up every now and then to be sure you take notice of her. You understand that. You were a middle child yourself. You were so good, sometimes I'd worry. You're good to me still.

Her mother looks up from sealing the piecrust over the apples and eyes Ethna with cunning. I've an idea for you for Christmas. I saw a lovely suit in the department store.

No, Ma, Ethna says. No.

Ma's Fashion Advice:

Don't be wearing those baggy tops and pants. Don't.

Did you go to work in that, honey? You're a manager now. You must have meetings and things. Do they not expect you to look the part?

You could dress that outfit up with a scarf and a nice brooch. Draw attention to your face. You've a lovely face. Any man would be lucky to have you.

This red jacket, now, would be good for you—a little color, and it's got nice shoulders, and it comes past your hips. Trimming. A tailored look is what you need.

Her ma describes all the wonders this suit would do for Ethna, and Ethna resists the temptation to tell her, Look! I've slept with a man! More than one! I've foiled your little plan my own way. And nobody at work gives a shit how I dress or how I write an SQL query, so long as when they sit down at the computer, I've found a way to make it go.

When Ethna's father comes in from the garage, the hairs rise on the back of her neck. She turns from the counter. She never stands with her back to him.

As soon as he pulls off his coat, Eamon complains that it's stifling inside. He goes to check the thermostat and comes back to the kitchen spitting and hissing at her ma. Did you touch it? How many times do I have to tell you it's on an automatic program? You'll ruin it. Ruin it. And we'll have no heat at all.

Rage seems to make him swell to gargantuan proportions even as it thins his voice, and if Ethna's not careful she'll be back in it, shaking, *in her place*, cringing even before his fist comes up. His body's a set of blunt instructions for her, still triggers recoil and a burning sensation in her skin. She was sixteen before it occurred to her to turn and run instead of standing there waiting to get it. Oh, to learn that escape was possible, him jumping the hedge out front to go after her, her mother standing by the door cradling her shame in her crossed arms while Ethna and her father flew around the yard, *out where all the neighbors could see*, till he caught her—*gotcha*—and hammered her on the third go-round.

I turned the heat up, Ethna says. I'm cold.

And will it be you paying the heating bill at the end of the month? he says. Do you think *click* I'm made of money?

Just tell me what you're charging, Ethna says. I'll write you a check before I leave.

He stands staring at her, fury temporarily filling out the flesh of his cheeks, his mouth flapping loose as he tries to come up with a reply.

Where's supper? he says finally.

It's hard to repress a smirk. Ethna wouldn't be gloating exactly. Occasionally she will go toe to toe with some honcho at work and then scoot back to her office and shut the door and giggle like a schoolgirl. It wouldn't be half as much fun if she actually believed a grown-up would listen to her. Her real self is still twelve.

Her father sits at the table to lecture her while he waits for his food. You'll have nothing but trouble with that car. That's what you get for your fancy airs.

They eat in silence. Ethna's mother takes small bites and chews them with grim effort; because of the paralyzed muscles in her throat she chokes on food unless she chews thoroughly. Across from her, Ethna's father plants his elbows on the table and hunches over his plate as if to guard it. He sloshes food in his mouth, gumming his dentures, wincing. Last summer when Ethna's mother had the stroke, he drove her to the hospital, parked the car, and left her there while he went in search of a wheelchair, no need to trouble anyone. Ethna doesn't think she wants revenge. Just a fair outcome: that illness should whittle him down as it has, winnow the available options for obstructing others.

Her mother looks up as if she has thought of something to say, or wants to think of something to say, only to smile apologetically at Ethna.

Something goes wrong again with the mechanics of Ethna's vision. It's as if the room has moved by faster than her eye has tracked, making her feel something like motion sickness. She blinks to clear her eyes. But everything in her field of vision still seems softly furred by the play of remnant light. She feels as if she could reach out and touch the velvety coating that's been laid over everything, from the plastic place mats on the table to her mother's soft nest of hair. Bringing her fork to her mouth—tentatively, uncertain now about where the edges of things really are—she is not surprised to find that the food slips smoothly down her throat, as if it's encased in a gelatinous sac. This must be what it's like to eat oysters. Not a pleasant sensation.

Ethna should take Sheila's advice and make an appointment with the optometrist. There's no advice of Sheila's in which Ethna doesn't hear her own voice, the back-and-forth of their mutual elaboration, an unfinished revision, a gleeful rivalry sustained for hours on the phone.

A Glossary of Tips:

How to Talk about Our Father: I had to tell the chair of the history department that I might need to fly home because my father was having heart surgery, and he says, I'm so sorry. And I have to pretend I'm sorry too. I'm not going to explain. I can't. *Here's what I do: When they say I'm sorry, I say, Don't be. I don't give a shit about the bastard. But my family might need me. After that, they don't ask you any questions.* Do you feel we were rooked? I do. I feel foolish for getting my hopes up. For thinking that something's gotta give.

How to Handle Your Professional Life: Explain this to me again, Ethna. You have this employee who's complaining about you behind your back to cover for her own incompetence, and you decide you can make her happy if you give her your corner office. *Don't you think, when you have the advantage of brains, you might as well be merciful? Butter wouldn't melt in her mouth now. And why do I care where I work? Just think, if I turned into one of those he-women who gloats over getting a corner office. It's mostly women working for me, and I tell them, as long as you do your job, you can come in when you want. Take your kid to the dentist and finish the data entry at night.*

How to Predict the Future: They can't manage in that house anymore. We're going to have to hire a landscaping service to do the yard. *I did that already. He chased the guy off. He's getting more cuckoo since the surgery. Now he doesn't want to pay the bills, he's been letting them pile up, and you know her. She's expecting the electricity to be shut off tomorrow.* We told her this was coming. We told her she couldn't even write a check for groceries if anything happened to him. Did you make sure they have their supplemental health insurance? I don't want Ma dependent on Medicare. If she gets really sick, he'll put her in some place where they tie you to the bed. *He'll pay for his own insurance, but not hers. It's seventy-eight bucks a month for her, and I figure we can split it. We're going to have to sit them down and tell them they have to move. Sean won't be much help, but he'll go along with us. We'll just tell Dad, look, we're taking her out of here if you don't straighten up. I have a room for her now.* We're never going to get her away from him. But if we could get them to sell the house and move into assisted living—I wonder if a mortgage company would write two checks for the sale, one to him and one to her. The house is the only thing that's in her name.

How to Weigh Alternatives: What do you mean, your vision goes blurry? How long have you had this? Why haven't you been to the optometrist? *Well, you know, at first I was entertaining the idea maybe this was some kind of special sign from God. Like maybe I should start going to church.* Now I'm really worried you've got a brain tumor. Isn't altered personality one of the signs? *Do you have to spoil my fun? Just when I was hoping maybe I'm going to start having visions. And I won't get cheesed off anymore when Ma asks me what she's going to do about paying the bills.* You deserve *some* reward. But that's beside the point. You have to take care of this. It could be something serious. *That would bring a bloom back to the cheeks of all the Irish friends and relations. They were jamming into Dad's hospital room every day, fighting for the best spot, soaking up all the excitement.* Don't have a brain tumor. I couldn't bear the world without you.

After dinner Ethna's ma fetches the prescription bottles from the cupboard. She doles out pills beside Eamon's plate, tells him what each of them is for. He says it's ridiculous, he's not taking six pills every night after dinner, and she repeats her explanations, You need it, see, for the fluid on your lungs.

Woman, would you quit your fussing? Eamon says. He turns to Ethna. You see what I have to put up with?

My heart bleeds for you, Ethna says.

He leaves the pills on the table and gets up and goes to the living room to sit and read the newspaper.

I don't know what to do with him, Ethna's ma says.

I should go, Ethna says. I still have work to do tonight.

She'll go home and call Sheila and deliver a full report on the status quo, because there's only Sheila to call, just like there's only Sheila to call when she's still giddy that she's managed to snag a guy: There's a man in my bed!

Her mother says, I don't like this habit you have of taking work home and staying up all hours of the night. You need to take better care of yourself, love.

They're hazy as dust motes, these wishes and hopes of her mother's, but still they swarm.

Ethna says, I'll go straight home and pull the covers up to my chin.

Before you go, would you help me out with this one thing? He says he's not going to pay the bills till I stop nagging him. And I put them on the counter there, and he's taken them and done something with them, and I know there's half of them past due.

Treasure hunt. Ethna does this with the kids when she has them all together, writes clues in the form of rhymes and has them race all over the house for chocolate coins, tiny combat figures, barrettes, little things that are still treats to them. She helps her mother search the kitchen, wincing as she opens dusty cupboards, flicks scabs of dried flour from the shelves, discovers jars of moldy jam. They sneak past her father in the living room to search his bureau drawers, and then her mother guesses that he might have hidden the bills in the basement. Ethna forbids her mother to follow her. She worries about her negotiating the rickety stairs every time she brings laundry down to the washing machine.

Ethna came down here last week on the same errand. Piles of junk have proliferated with bacterial profusion, like the dust clumps and crumbs in all the corners upstairs where her mother can't reach because if she leans over she'll topple and she's got holes in her head if she thinks he's going to pay someone to come in to do cleaning. There are boxes scattered everywhere, spilling plaid blankets and wool jackets and water-stained pillows, and a foldaway cot and broken chairs and tools too heavy for her father to carry up the stairs anymore and a rack of clothes her parents haven't worn for years, smelling of mildew. How infinite a job it will be to clear this out when they get their parents to sell the house.

It's so hard to say no when her mother is wringing her hands, but if the gas and electricity got shut off, that might be the last little push they need. Ethna halfheartedly searches her father's workbench, dusty and spiderwebbed, laden with tools and odd spare parts that might still do service, everything in a place where he can find it. Screws he could have kept in paper sacks are sorted by size in baby-food jars, their lids nailed to the rafter above the bench so he can reach up to twist free the jar he wants.

Some similarly copious economy must dictate the hiding place for the bills, but Ethna can't guess at it. In her tour of the basement she discovers the sewer pump, dismantled, and gets a little shock: sure, they know he's crazy, but this crazy? Still searching in the pipes for those dentures? It's gibberish only in the way that the SQL queries she writes are indecipherable to the uninitiated. No gear could have sprung loose in the workings of him, who put everything to use, who made Ethna sweep small piles of sawdust from beneath the workbench to be pitchforked into the compost heap, fine particles escaping into the air, stirred into invisibility by her effort.

Commands for Adding Tablespaces:

```
SQL> create tablespace TOOLS;
SQL> create tablespace APPL_TAB datafile size 250M;
SQL> create tablespace APPL_TDX datafile size 250M;
SQL> create tablespace USERS
2 datafile '/u02/olendata/users/01.dbf' size 5M;
SQL> select tablespace_name, file_name, bytes
2 from dba_data_files;
```

Her father will have some reason, but still Ethna feels queasy, as if she's intruded on someone obscenely naked. When she entered her father's hospital room after his surgery, his body had been turned inside out to expose all its functions—the ventilator compressing his lungs, the IV pumping what should have flowed secretly in his veins, the catheter snaking from his groin to a clear plastic sack. When he fretted at the sheets, Ethna glimpsed even the ribbed pouches of his balls. All right, she'd expected something, felt some strange hope that this suffering, this humiliation of the body, promised what she had been waiting for all her life. Some crashing through. No. It was what her mother had been waiting for all her life. Her mother fussed shamelessly over her father in the bed, swabbed his dry, cracked lips with a Q-tip dipped in Vaseline, jumped to untangle tubes whenever the IV monitor beeped, kept tugging the sheets over his exposed, stringy thigh. He's weak as a kitten, her mother said tenderly.

Ethna hears a noise on the stairs and thinks it's him, thinks he's remembered that he has to reconnect the sewer pump. But then she hears a thump, a little squeal of terror, and the thud-thud-thud that shuts off protest. She runs to find her mother sprawled at the bottom of the stairs, facedown.

A jolt of longing.

The first surge of sympathy indistinct from this impatience to be done with it.

Ethna draws in a breath as if to prompt her mother to do the same and chokes on the dust-laden air, the sour odor of decay, the stillness that begs her to act.

Her mother moans.

God, it's difficult lifting even a small woman, figuring out where to grasp her mother's frail body, how to bend knees and elbows in order to heft her to a sitting position on the stairs.

I hit my head, her mother says dully.

A bump has already popped up on her ma's forehead. Her right forearm looks lumpy near the wrist. Awry. Ethna asks her mother to open and close her fist, to test whether she can move her legs without pain. A broken hip would put her in a nursing home. Her mother starts to cry softly.

Concussion? Broken arm? Ethna tries to remember what she learned in the first-aid course she took a few years ago, in case she'd ever need it for the kids. She searches for information in the massive index that is her brain, with the same lucid persistence with which she tracks down problems in the database at work.

First Aid for Suspected Fractures:
Elevate the affected limb.
Apply ice to the area at twenty-minute intervals.
To immobilize the limb, a splint can be fashioned from a cardboard tube or a tightly rolled shirt. Care must be taken not to bind the limb too tightly.

I have to take you to the emergency room, Ethna says.

No, no, her mother whispers.

I'm going to get you some ice for that arm. It will numb the pain.

But her mother loops the fingers of her left hand through Ethna's, holds her there.

Ethna hears the hacking sound of her father's breathing before she looks up to see him at the top of the stairs.

What have you done now? he says.

I fell, her mother says.

You did *what?* he says.

Ethna's mother weeps.

Ethna says, I think Ma broke her arm.

Eamon zeroes in on his wife. You're the only one of us can drive, and you have to be so careless. You've ruined everything.

For a moment he is mercilessly turned inside out again. For a moment Ethna is remembering last week's hunt in the basement, the letter she found in the rafter above his bench, addressed to his sister in Dublin when he never even signed his name to birthday cards. She should have left that letter untouched in its hiding place.

> Hello Noreen, I am a little slow but getting there. I am up and around every day so I can't gripe too much. Nothing to complain of unless you count my kids. You would like to disown the whole bunch not a one of them cares. I don't let it bother me as life is too short.

Nothing, nothing to complain of when he was shivering in his hospital bed, and Ethna offered to fetch a blanket, and he roused himself and in a drugged voice ordered her not to go troubling the nurses for no reason. Just as there had been no need to trouble anyone when he drove her mother to the hospital.

No need.

In the narrow rectangle at the top of the stairs, Eamon's looming big man's body eclipses the light. There's only a thin silvery edging to the flat disk of him. Ethna stares up at her father for too long. A dull ache presses at the back of her eyes, shimmering her vision, weirdly beautiful, terrifying.

Because the only other choice is ruin.

Much Have I Traveled

When Leslie offered help with dinner, Nina politely demurred. Leslie had already changed into a swimsuit, and Nina would turn down even a serious offer. She ruled alone over the kitchen once they arrived here for the summer, and every day she drove down the mountain to fetch groceries in town, negotiating the hairpin curves of a dirt road that wound through stands of redwoods. She planned the menu only when she saw what was fresh at the farmers' market and then devoted the afternoon to cooking. Nina had inherited the property eight years ago, remnant of a sizable tract of family wealth that had dwindled steadily over two generations. The sturdy old house had three bedrooms, and out back stood a decaying shed, with plank walls so chipped and rotted that it was only a matter of time until it collapsed. The guests who came and went all summer were encouraged to follow Nina and Carter's example and make their own amusement. During the day some of them worked in that porous shed. They might write, like Carter, or huddle out there with a guitar, or spend the hours reading.

Mitch and Carter were absorbed in the map laid out on the kitchen table, but Leslie dawdled, trying to persuade one of them to come with her to the pond. Over her swimsuit, she wore the cotton man's shirt she worked in, scabbed with dried bits of clay, just like her hands and arms. She had claimed the shed. When she and Aaron arrived from Oregon, plastic bags of clay packed in the bed of their truck, she announced in a tone of warning that she was a ceramicist, not a potter. Carter snickered.

When he looked up at Leslie still in the doorway, Carter said, I only swim naked. Can I still come?

Leslie stole a look at Nina, but Nina offered only a smile.

Didn't Aaron tell you there's no need for a swimsuit here? Carter said. Or is he anxious to protect your virtue?

Aaron and Carter had been friends for decades, but Leslie was Aaron's second wife, a newcomer. She beat a hasty retreat, unaware that this would please Carter every bit as much as watching her shuck her swimsuit. It was all foreplay to him.

When Leslie had hopped out of that truck, her rolled-up shirtsleeves showing off her tanned, well-muscled arms, Carter had whispered to Nina, *permission slip.* They used to say this to one another even when they felt only a hypothetical flicker of lust. Cynical Carter was susceptible to flirtation. No more ridiculous than the standard heterosexual hang-up on monogamy and the nasty attendant jealousy. He didn't want to put her through that, but there'd be opportunities, always opportunities when he traveled to give lectures or readings, and she was entitled too. Nina had married him so young; she'd longed to rise to that seemingly impossible demand. But it turned out not to be so difficult: in agreeing to his terms she'd leached flirtation of some of its enticing uncertainty.

While Nina pitted cherries for a clafouti, Mitch talked over with Carter his trip to Baja. Carter spent a year there, long ago. When he left them, Mitch would drive down the coast, but not before he sounded Carter on every allurement. Which maybe explained Carter's keen interest in Leslie. He had to scratch that itch on *something*.

Mitch planned to live out of his car. Camp on beaches. Fish for dinner.

Strip back to the essentials, he said. I even tossed my furniture.

The furniture and the teaching job Carter finagled for him after his first book came out. Mitch had the sweet idea that this wholehearted abdication was the required antidote for a stubborn case of writer's block. Nina's fingertips were inked with juice stains because it pleased her to do what was not in any way necessary, but she turned from the counter to say, It can't hurt to try.

Even Carter granted a special dispensation to the truly, truly earnest. There's no harm in superstition, he said. These old guys I knew in the merchant marine, they believed pigs can't drown. They all had tattoos of pigs on the soles of their feet.

I don't know what else to do, Mitch said.

Carter shrugged. It's not usually helpful to whine.

A lot of people took Carter's pronouncements to heart. The obstinate success of his former students had done more for his reputation than his own slender output of short stories. He warned students that the work was brutal, would take too much from them, and they signed on in droves. Nina had preceded Mitch by a few years in Carter's writing workshops. Like Mitch, she fell in love with Carter's lacerating intelligence, his casual disdain for his students. She was used to coddling from her teachers, and here was the man to burn off any remnant need.

Mitch tapped the map. What about Loreto? On the Sea of Cortez.

Carter said, 'Much have I traveled in the realms of gold, and many goodly states and kingdoms seen.'

Mitch frowned.

Keats, Nina said. 'On First Looking into Chapman's Homer.' It's too hard to explain the poem. But Cortez is in it, looking at the Pacific as if he owns it.

Only that's a mistake, Carter said. A real beauty. It was Balboa who discovered the Pacific.

Mitch tapped the map again. I was hoping for some practical help.

When I was in Loreto, Carter said, you could wade out into the Sea of Cortez to fish with nothing but a spoon tied to a nylon line for bait, and you'd reel in a grouper the length of your arm. This was before it was overfished.

Carter could tell stories—the stint in the merchant marine and so much else in his itinerant youth—but if Nina still believed he could talk about anything, she had never seen any of this for herself. When she married him twelve years ago, she was twenty-one, and he was forty. An associate professor, and his friends also professors, serious people secure in their careers, whose respect for him impressed her but constituted yet another kind of secondhand knowledge.

Mitch said, I hear the islands off Loreto are still pretty much untouched. You can haul your boat out of the water and sleep on the beach. I might take a kayak.

You are counting on this trip for too much, Carter said.

You should come with me, Mitch said. Even for a couple of weeks.

Maybe I will, Carter said.

He didn't even look at Mitch but cast a hopeful glance at the clock on the stove. Strict now about when he started drinking, Carter had postponed by an hour the time when he reeled in their guests to sit on the porch with a bottle of scotch.

Nina turned to face Mitch. What's the temperature like in Baja in the summer?

It gets up in the hundreds in July and August.

Nina said to Carter, And you complain about the heat here.

In the mountains above Santa Cruz, summer days averaged seventy degrees, and nights were deliciously cool. Carter went barefoot all summer. Even in winter, he wore short-sleeved shirts and sandals.

Carter stood unsteadily. I'm going to fetch Aaron, he said.

Nina waited for him to go. Then she said, He can't take heat anymore.

Oh, Mitch said. You forget. He's made such a fight of it.

Carter inspired surprising loyalty. Former students issued invitations to read at the colleges where they taught, or if they had taken his advice and pursued a sensible career, shared their success in Christmas letters and proffered the keys to vacation homes in Hawaii. Nina, only marginally sensible, got a degree in library science and went to work at a university that gave her summers off with Carter. She was as happy deliberating over book catalogs as she was reading the novels and plays and critical studies she ordered. Pure plunder.

I don't know if you should dangle that trip in front of him, Nina said.

It must be tough on you, Mitch said. I mean, he'd never stand for it. You turning yourself into a nursemaid.

Nina laughed. That's not in the cards.

Another sweet notion, but the situation called for nothing so romantic. Four years ago, Carter went to the doctor because he thought drinking was giving him tremors, blurring his vision. Probably the MS was subtly active long before he registered its effects—as a student Nina had admired that off-balance walk of his, sexy as his crooked grin. Multiple sclerosis stripped nerves of their myelin sheath only randomly, countered by the body's mechanisms for compensation. The consequences were unpredictable and intermittent, impossible to forecast, difficult to diagnose, but Carter appeared to have only a mild form of the disease. He might never require a wheelchair, and he would most likely die of some other cause.

When Carter failed to return with Aaron—and by seven, the liberation promised by the clock lured Nina as powerfully as it did Carter—Nina went to get them. She stopped at the door of Aaron and Leslie's bedroom, where Aaron worked on a laptop for the better part of the day. He wrote biographies, thank God, nothing to whet Carter's appetite for competition.

Nina didn't mean to eavesdrop, but as she raised her fist to knock, she heard Carter speak. Just a phrase, guttural with vindictiveness. *On me like a gluttonous schoolmarm.*

He could be speaking about Mitch. Nothing to do with her. Still, it provoked the same eerie longing she experienced when she listened to him tell stories, this partial glimpse triggering a lush arousal.

From among all the beautiful girls who flocked to his classes, Carter had singled out Nina, only passably a pretty little thing.

She'd kept the long blond hair, but their marriage was about another kind of excitement. Their extraordinary bargain. He'd loomed so large on the horizon of her little world when she met him—her English professor who could quote anything chapter and verse, sonorously invoking the Bible or lecherously reciting Shakespeare, a real *writer*, so much sexier and more disreputable than a mere teacher—that she was happy to let him pocket her youth if he would fill her coffers in exchange.

Nina woke to the sound of Carter calling her name with compressed urgency. She pushed back the covers and knelt at his feet, her butt resting on her heels, to clamp her hands over his ankles. He took in stride the bouts of double vision that limited his time at the computer. But sometimes he woke convinced he couldn't see. Usually only one eye went blank for a moment, but Carter believed the darkness would encroach. He never declared this fear; he might lie rigid for an hour in its wake.

The firm contact of Nina's hands on his numb feet countered the sensation that he couldn't locate his body parts, anchored him, teased him back toward possession of himself.

He wrote only at night now, hunching over the glowing laptop in the dark, attempting to revive some hunger for his old habit. Nina worried that working in dim light triggered these visual disturbances, but then again, maybe it was easier on his eyes. They never discussed whether these episodes were psychological or symptomatic.

She yawned. Soon she'd be shivering in the cold room. He slept naked, and this body that sometimes seemed to slip away from him remained lean and taut, as smoothly muscled as a thirty-year-old's. In another ten years she would look as old as he did, if she was very lucky in what aging did to her more susceptible female flesh.

After a while Carter started to talk. He needed to talk, to size and master this physical humiliation with his mind. He said the ancient Greeks so feared blindness that they construed it as a savage gift. None of the blind seers ever foretold good news. Only damaging truths.

With her thumbs Nina applied steady pressure to the arches of his feet. They had a taste for that, she said. The hero is always crippled.

The hero is always punished, Carter said. Odysseus makes it home after all his travels, he's redeemed by his wife waiting for him and his son who's so enthusiastic about the mayhem they have to conduct to erase his absence. They couldn't just slaughter all the suitors. Telemachus had to hang the maids who served them, string them up by the neck, all together, 'hung like doves.' Homer insists you have to look—it's beautiful, their brutality. Odysseus retrieves everything only because he does not flinch, and years later he dies anyway at the hand of his own son, his other abandoned son, his child by Circe. Telegonus, I think. Telemachus, Telegonus. Same root: *tele*. Far off. What's far off always comes for you in the end.

She loved these devious riffs of his, the way they arrived at some dissonant absolute statement. He might or might not mock you if you fell for it. Carter never wanted to get caught being sincere, but even so—when she was his student he'd made her feel she'd embarked on something important. In their conferences, which Carter required even of students he treated to blithe sarcasm in class, he prefaced the drubbing he was about to give her by saying, You won't let this hold you back.

I think Mitch lusts after you, Carter said.

Nina massaged his feet. They had become the most intimately known part of his body for her, the swirled ridges of his calluses, the crooked toes that curled tightly at her touch, the tender protrusion of a vein over bone.

You don't see the way he looks at you? Carter said. The lovely wife. With your beautiful manners.

When they began their affair, Carter honorably banished her from his classes. Nina had feared he would tire of her soon. So many others waited in the wings. She must be an embarrassment among his friends, so thrilled, so eager. His divorce from his first wife had just become final. Jean had been a student of his too, and the gossip among Nina's classmates thoroughly rendered how his wife had suffered over his flirtations, public scenes and ultimatums until she left him for someone her own age. *Jean, Jean, Jean,* Nina would say viciously to herself, a reminder, a punishment, a promise of defeat. Nina might still be that terrified girl if Carter had not freed her.

Is this about Leslie? Nina said.

I cleared that with you already, Carter said.

She and Carter had partnered tonight against Leslie and Aaron in a game of darts on the back porch, and Leslie couldn't keep her hands off Aaron. Maybe that was intended for an audience. For boisterous Carter, who kept overshooting the mark, his trembling hand pinging darts into the wall, embedded so deeply they had to be wrenched out with the claw of a hammer.

Neither of them had asked for permission in a long time. Carter had been amused when he first began to have trouble getting it up, another random inroad made by his disease, and even more amused when he came home from the doctor with a prescription for four Viagra a month, the maximum his health insurance would cover. Only the headaches the Viagra gave him could persuade him to concede to this limit. An unfair advantage to her, when he must count out his opportunities.

Not here, Nina said. It's pretty cramped quarters.

She doesn't strike me as the type to get carried away, Carter said. And anyway, she'll be gone in a week.

This was all just talk. Leslie seemed well matched with Aaron, had the same canny alertness, barricaded behind a courteous reserve. She seemed willing to amuse herself while Aaron spent his days working. As much as Carter loved the idea of not being able to help himself, he wasn't impulsive. To get it right (bittersweet, transient, unencumbered) mattered more to him than getting results, and if a crush did not pan out he conceded without regret. It was the same with his work: so few stories survived their prolonged gestation.

And what if Aaron catches you? Nina said.

You don't think I can do it, Carter said. You don't think I have any tricks left up my sleeve.

But they were in on it together. Carter, slamming darts into the wall, grinning, warning Leslie and Aaron they'd better stand behind the door, was just trying to shake up the competition so he and Nina could win. He still trusted her as his first reader, arguing with her over sentences, nodding grimly when she found fault. He had not downgraded his estimate of her when she gave up writing early on. Too many people, he said, wanted to be writers just because they had talent.

Nina returned her hands to Carter's ankles. You think you can sleep now?

When he didn't answer, she scrambled over his legs and crawled back toward her pillow, her calves protesting their prolonged compression. She pulled the covers up to her neck, but he peeled them back, caressed the knob of her shoulder with a touch lighter than hers on the dense flesh of his feet. His hand drifted to her back, skating up and down her spine until it elicited tingles.

He made such an effort to be inventively erotic, to circumvent the imposed limit. He wanted to take long baths together, soap and shave her legs, holding her foot snug against his penis while he drew the razor down her calf, or walk into the woods with a blanket and work on her while the barrier of her clothing remained intact. He told her, This is turning out to be a good deal for you. He expected her to return his touch with the same lascivious intent, though it would not result in any orgasm for him.

Carter slipped his hand to her breast, and Nina rolled onto her back to wait out his slow progress toward her crotch.

Maybe Carter had guessed right about Mitch. He hung around in the kitchen all afternoon, watching Nina prepare a butterflied leg of lamb, rolled around stuffing studded with artichokes, mushrooms, and black olives. Once she set the roasting pan in the oven, she agreed to go with him down to the pond. They threw towels over their shoulders and headed out the back door. The path led past the shed, its warped and shredded walls riddled with chinks, and through these crevices Nina could make out Carter and Leslie, standing close together, rippling the light every time they moved. The eroding structure granted such fragmented access that she couldn't be too sure what she saw.

She heard Leslie scold Carter in a tone of exaggerated amusement. Not with your *thumb*, Leslie said.

Nina paused for only a second before moving on.

Mitch fell into step beside her and said, Leslie let me have a look too. She's making these tiny little buildings, lopsided minarets made of this white clay. Like something out of a Disney movie. She's got a whole city set up in there. You should get her to show you.

Nina could have kicked herself for hesitating.

I hope Aaron is working very hard today, she said.

Carter can be mean, Mitch said.

And this comes as a surprise to you? she said.

Yesterday she had fielded Leslie's veiled attempt to ascertain whether she grasped the rules of Nina's marriage. Rules that Carter had apparently suspended: by rights he should have told Nina if his interest had gone beyond speculation.

She had botched it the first time she took a lover, running home to Carter to confide in his arms, in bed. Only a week before she'd been begging him for the same, and he wouldn't cough up the gory details of a sexual conquest on his last trip. Carter listened to Nina deliver the goods and then released her and sat on the edge of the bed. You amaze me, he said. She thought he wanted more from her. He had to put a hand over her mouth to stop her. Do I tell you everything? he said. There's no need to hurt each other. She had to learn to collude with him not only in the exercise of this prerogative but in the delicate transaction of reporting the event without confessing it.

Nina plucked sorrel from beneath a tree, a tiny furled umbrella of leaves, and told Mitch to bite the stem. He made a face when the bitter juices filled his mouth.

Carter likes to pull this trick on people, Nina said. It has the same aftertaste as semen. In case you've never sampled it.

Mitch spat. I expected better from you, he said, and they both laughed. Safely past that awkward moment of witness.

They emerged from the trees to stand on the grassy banks of the pond, still furrowed by the tracks of wheelbarrows. When the pond became clotted with algae scum a few years ago, the channel from the creek slowly filling in, Nina had accepted this next small loss, the pond growing murky the way her memories of summers here as a child had silted up over time. They couldn't really afford to keep up the property that had come to her, and they could not pay to dredge the pond. But Carter started digging a new channel from the creek and enlisted their guests in daily labor, flinging stinking muck on the grass, scoring the earth with shovels, tearing rocks from the creek bed and carting them in wheelbarrows to line the raw trench. When Nina saw what he'd done, they fought. I don't want this, she said. You will when you get to swim again, he said confidently. Every day she would feel sick imagining his devastating progress. Every day he would return to the house as fully used up as she had ever seen him, exhausted and cocky and alert. All that summer she stayed out of the woods.

Nina and Mitch settled near a cluster of bushes to strip off their clothes. Nina took the clip from her ponytail and shook out her hair. When she pulled her T-shirt over her head, Mitch turned away from her to undress, folding his shirt carefully and hanging it over a bush to screen himself from view. His modesty aroused her even more than the working of the muscles in his back. She hadn't taken a lover in years. She didn't need to, once she'd proved to Carter that she wouldn't be the wronged party, the weepy little girl.

Nina shucked her jeans while Mitch hesitated over the zipper of his pants.

It was excruciating to watch him put off stripping, as if it portended so much. Nina scrambled out of her underwear and ran for the pond. She gasped when she hit the cold water and then dove in headfirst. She had swum out to deep water by the time Mitch joined her.

In the water he shed his timidity. He splashed her. He let his eyes drift to her breasts. He plucked at the strands of her hair floating on the surface of the water and let them glide through his fingers. She had forgotten how desire took the form of hazy fumbling, forgotten it was possible not to feel like a woman submitting to a voyeur watching at the window, forced to hide her awareness of his intent observation.

Mitch planted his feet to stand, water funneling down the sharp central divide of his chest. Through the cloudy water, Nina could see his penis bobbing against his leg. Halfway to upright.

Carter claims he's serious about coming with me to Mexico, Mitch said. He told me not to tell you. He said you worry more than you should.

That's not how he put it, Nina said.

From what I can see, he doesn't have any grounds for complaint.

Nina could feel Mitch's desire to kiss her, if she would just hold still for it.

I really want to do it for him, Mitch said. Whatever it takes. OK by me if it's not easy.

Wrong gambit.

Nina shrugged. He'll insist he can drive.

Mitch's hand grazed her hip beneath the water. I know. I know he's lying about that too.

What must Carter have said about her to fire this ardor?

But if he can't, Mitch said. If you don't want him to go. Tell me.

Oh, the sweet, hankering flutter of nerves in the wake of his hand. Oh, the temptation, passing like a shadow on the water, to tell him Carter's depth perception was shot and his vision blurred and his stamina in shreds. Rat the bastard out.

If he wants to go, take him, Nina said.

With a little flutter kick she pulled away from Mitch.

Mitch and Carter hid in the kitchen with Nina, waiting for Leslie and Aaron to finish shouting and throwing things. They had shut the kitchen door to muffle the noise, and Nina had just laid a sheet of fresh pasta dough to rest on the counter, and she had peas to shell, mushrooms to clean, but she found it hard to ignore the rise and fall of angry voices, punctuated by the sound of her possessions being hurled across the room.

They'd started in not long after she got back from the market. She didn't know if Aaron had actually caught Leslie and Carter in the act or glimpsed a kiss or badgered an admission from his wife. They couldn't seem to just toss their things in a suitcase and leave. They marched back and forth from the bedroom to the living room, out to their truck and back, cursing each other with vigor when their paths crossed. Aaron's self-possession had always made Nina feel she didn't really know him. Now she listened to him call his wife a slut and a bitch and rage at her in a teary voice.

Nina set the colander of pea pods on the table before the two men. You might as well work for your supper, she said.

Mitch shelled peas with the alacrity of a guilty party. Carter watched him work industriously for a while and then sloppily fished out a handful of pea pods. When they fell through his fingers to his lap, he fumbled for them.

Under the circumstances it would be assuming too much to suspect he was heading for a relapse. The warning signs did not follow a set pattern—he might have a bad day or spend a week in bed, shaking feverishly. But the body improvised in the wake of disaster; the nerve cells strove to regenerate their insulating myelin sheath, accruing scar tissue, or cunningly produced alternate routes for transmitting nerve impulses.

The door to the kitchen swung open and Aaron strode in to kick, once, hard, at Carter's chair.

You son of a bitch, Aaron said. After twenty years of friendship.

He swept the colander from the table, sending peas skittering across the floor. The door banged behind him when he left.

On their way back to Oregon he and Leslie would have to drive for hours, be forced to share a motel room for the night. For the first time Nina worried if Leslie was safe with Aaron.

I'll drive her to town, Nina said. She can take the bus. She can't go with him.

Mitch had crouched on the floor to scoop peas back into the colander. He looked up at Nina. If it comes to that, I'll take her.

No one has to do anything, Carter said. They're all right. Stay out of it.

Again Leslie and Aaron crossed paths in the living room. She yelled at him this time. You think you didn't give me any reason?

Nina was making up her mind to go out there and get between them when Leslie's voice suddenly dropped in register. Distinctly and calmly, she said, Don't forget that book you left out on the porch.

Aaron made some muffled reply. Then the front door slammed, and a few moments later, the truck started.

Nina wondered what came next. Would they drive in silence for hours, or argue? Would she remind him to turn on the headlights at dusk? Would they wait to take up their fight again until after they pulled off the highway to find a motel? Would they cry in each other's arms and then be too ashamed to take off their clothes in front of one other? Would they make love in the same old way or some new one, trespass always a part of it or only every now and then clanking along behind them like a can tied to the tail of some hapless dog?

Carter scraped his chair back from the table. Nina followed him out to the living room to tally her losses: books swept from the shelves and a cracked ceramic lamp, a shattered lightbulb and chips of clay ground into the Soumak carpet her grandmother had given her when she married. Oh, and if Carter had dipped into his supply of Viagra, one less night of real sex for her this month.

Nina felt a sharp sense of injury. But she was hardly entitled.

Carter sank onto the sofa and put his hand over his eyes. I'm sorry, he said. I made a bad call. I thought she was an adult. But she wanted him to catch her.

Why hadn't he told Nina? Why get sloppy now?

From the kitchen Mitch hollered that he was getting a broom.

Nina went to stop him from volunteering.

You don't have to do that, she said.

He came to her and put his arms around her. She stiffened, embarrassed, conscious of the ticking of his heart beneath his shirt. She could feel his intention to kiss her, the way she had at the pond.

Why do you put up with his crap? Mitch said hoarsely. He goes out of his way to insult you. *Leslie.* With her idiotic little grammar-school project. You're still young. And he's done. Old and sick and mean. You must feel—just *had* by him.

He meant to romance her, so certain his solace would be welcome.

Nina was about to knock his arms aside when Carter came into the kitchen, his right foot slapping the floor, that off-note in his walk.

Feel free, Carter said. Don't let me interrupt.

Carter's foot was bleeding. He had tramped through the broken glass in his bare feet, and he might not even know he'd cut himself.

I'm going to the pond, Mitch said, his voice shaking with rage. You should come with me, Nina, but I don't expect you will.

No, she wouldn't be taking him up on his invitation.

Sit down, Nina said to Carter. I have to clean that cut on your foot.

At the door, Mitch told her she could always change her mind.

Nina wet a dish towel at the sink and knelt before Carter. Propping his foot on her knee, she gently wrung water from the dish towel to wash away the smeared blood. The cut looked superficial. When she probed the skin for filaments of glass, Carter did not wince.

Don't pass up a good thing on my account, Carter said. He'd worship you. Wouldn't you like that?

He's too serious, Nina said. He'd want me to run away with him.

Carter laughed. Oh, don't worry. He'd be held in check by the pathetic vision of me shuffling around on a cane.

Carter was not careless. He scrupulously severed ego from his work, resigned himself to futile, obscure effort. No. He would never say resigned. He would say devoted, disciplined. He would say his choice to submit to, not inflict, this ruthlessness. The bastard. The ingenious bastard, going out of his way to insult her.

Nina compressed the cloth on the wound to stanch the bleeding. She said, I'm going to get some disinfectant for this. You can't risk an infection.

Carter jeered at her. For God's sake. It's just a cut.

She met his eyes. Right, she said. Not worth the trouble.

He gripped her fiercely by the shoulders, and her breath caught in anticipation.

He pulled her head down to his lap. He called her name. He undid the clip that held her hair back and fanned her hair and called for her again.

The patience and shamming required of her lay so far off from the suffering she once longed for and lived within. That striving little girl, going to the annual faculty party just for a last chance to stalk him, to win from him some acknowledgment. She had an invitation only because the department wanted to honor a handful of students who'd been awarded prizes that year. In their increasingly long conferences in his office, Carter had given no sign of more than paternal interest in her. In a few days she would return home for the summer. For most of the night he ignored her, his star pupil—too busy attending to a pretty female colleague—and she realized she was going to burst into tears in the middle of that convivial crowd.

Carter was only half right about her impeccable manners. Nina left the party rather than make a scene. She stole his jacket from the closet and slipped into it for the walk to her dorm, free to let the tears come once she was alone. In the same way that she had unerringly chosen his jacket from among all the others, he had been acutely attuned to her departure. He caught up to her in the street. He said, I believe that's my coat you've got there. She was so young she imagined she knew how to make this stop. She shed the jacket easily and held it out to him. Take it, then, she said. He took it. He crammed it under his arm. He unbuttoned his shirtsleeve. Pulling the cuff over his hand, he swiped at her slick cheek. She jerked her head and caught his thumb in her mouth and bit down hard.

Seven Remedies

There should be more fuss, some bold stroke by which the gods announce their interference. But every day begins the same way. One of the guys on the construction crew rings the bell at 7:30 A.M., when Laurel is still in her robe, and she has to run to the bedroom to get dressed. By the time Laurel or Sam coaxes their two kids out the door to school, with Nathan swearing and slamming doors, as reluctant as his mother to face the day, the workers are already pounding at the massive beams that hold up the house, the exposed wood like blackened onionskin, soft and flaked by rot. The dismantling of the back wall has cracked what little Sheetrock remains, so the rooms look as if they've been bombed, their walls pocked with holes and seamed by zigzagging cracks, the air itself chalked by dust, visible, swarming each time a hammer bangs the wall.

Their new routine dictates that if one parent takes the girls to school, the other stays behind to exchange questions with the crew's foreman, all having to do with industrious making: they must decide whether to reinforce or re-pour the foundation; the foreman recommends double-paned vinyl tilt packs to replace the windows in the rotten back wall; Laurel and Sam must choose another tile for the demolished upstairs bathroom because their first choice doesn't come in bullnoses and quarter rounds. A part of Laurel loves this expanding universe of newly named things. A part of her feels like Gulliver being tied down by the aggregate force of a thousand minutiae. The deliberation, repeated anew each day, with irrelevant changes in the particulars, acquires the shape of an epigram: desire drives nothing in this world, only scurries within the cage of the possible.

Every day for two months Laurel has been late for work. When she gets to her office—a cubicle shared with other part-time faculty in the freshman writing program—she'll find she left something necessary at home, most likely because she was backing out the door while the crew foreman was still talking. When Laurel and Sam bought the house, they planned to use the basement room, now gutted, as an office for Laurel. They hired a contractor to make a few repairs before they moved in, and on the second day of work a ladder punched through the floor in the basement. It became a joke: every day Sam and Laurel would come by the house and ask cheerily, Any more bad news for us? Yes, there was, more and more: the cracked foundation, the basement floor of waterlogged particle board slapped on dirt, the myriad leaks sprung by the house, the discovery of wood-boring beetles and termites in those rotten beams. There was a certain thrill to this, the first real whopper of their married life.

Laurel and Sam have always lived so carefully, so modestly. In their old house, one of those tract houses that Joni Mitchell sang about, *ticky-tacky boxes*, they could save money, had the buffer of that pre-boom investment in San Francisco real estate. But Emma was ten and Nathan thirteen and they needed their own bedrooms; the grandparents shouldn't have to bunk in a kid's room when they visited; Laurel and Sam had earned this prerogative of middle age; why couldn't they have a little charm? When Nathan surveyed the room that would be his, he said, It's just a bigger box. Laurel and Sam weren't suspicious at all: they were unrolling a new Heriz carpet in the still bare living room when the foreman's ladder crashed through the soggy basement floor.

The foreman was not hurt in the fall, and anything hovering on the periphery of that luck—Laurel knows where she's supposed to look. When her parents left Germany as newlyweds in 1938, they arrived in Los Angeles with only the permitted personal goods (five silver fish forks and a dozen ruby-red, etched crystal wineglasses used once a year for the seder, nothing that would translate into cash). Greta and Henry lived each day with an exquisitely circumscribed hedonism, payment on a debt. Those glasses, along with vases and china salvaged from their past, were shattered in the Northridge earthquake a few years ago, and Laurel's mother only shrugged. While Laurel and Sam were house-hunting on Sunday afternoons, Greta was striving to keep secret Henry's deterioration. She meant to protect him, the paterfamilias, but she also bought them maybe a year in which his Alzheimer's disease was not yet a tangible threat. Greta would hate for Laurel to make a lesson of this: the art of pleasure lies in not being wary.

Laurel makes coffee for Mayda, who comes to clean house on Tuesday mornings. Laurel has to make up for lost time at work, so she doesn't sit with Mayda the way she usually does, but she stands at the counter to talk for at least a few minutes, ritual observed for twelve years, though Mayda doesn't speak English and Laurel speaks a present-tense-only, smacked-together Spanish. Funny what topics they are willing to trust to uncertainty: flowers, weather, children, parents. Laurel cheats, plucking from memory a Latin root that might serve both languages and inflecting it hopefully, which is as hit-or-miss as her efforts to convey sympathy for troubles with immigration—which touches on *parents*, her parents—or phrase questions about the teenaged daughter Mayda left in Oaxaca. That topic's better understood from the attention Mayda pays to Laurel's kids, bashful, alert, wondering.

Today it's Mayda and not the foreman who holds Laurel back. Mayda has been having terrible headaches. She's made a series of visits to the clinic at San Francisco General, where they don't make appointments but do see patients without health insurance. She missed work three times before they could tell her she had a benign pituitary tumor, a diagnosis she pantomimed for Laurel by circling her hand at the base of her skull.

Now Mayda sits at the table holding out to Laurel a prescription bottle, her face a virtual map of the difficulty they're about to face. Laurel manages to understand that Mayda called the clinic to report that the medicine they prescribed made her sick to her stomach, and they told her to take aspirin. It wouldn't help if the instructions on the bottle were written in Spanish; Mayda can't read in any language. Laurel had to drive her from their old house to the new house twice, so she could memorize the landmarks by which she'd find her way: *right turn after the yellow house, second left after the light, there's the bus stop.*

Over the years Mayda has worked for them, Sam and Laurel have loaned her money (once two thousand dollars, only two thousand, to buy a house in Oaxaca for her parents and her child), and Laurel has lied on notarized statements to help Mayda get her green card and written letters to Mayda's other clients to ask for a raise. Inequity requires excessive courtesy, more from Mayda than from Laurel. Because Laurel always makes coffee when she arrives, Mayda delays ringing the bell until after the frantic effort to get the kids off to school, and if her bus is early she waits on the sidewalk. She is copiously sympathetic about all the problems with their new house, all the troubles of ownership. When need forces its crude gestures on her—that proffered bottle—she makes her request brief and literal, preserving the barrier of distance by using the formal *usted*, referring to Laurel as *un buen patrón*.

Laurel calls a friend who is a psychiatrist. Lately Laurel has been asking too many favors of Abeer, who has coached Laurel through the intricacies of finding medication for her father. He reached his nineties without ever needing more than the occasional antibiotic. But his disease is in its end stages, a sudden tumble only if you forget how cunningly Greta staved off admission.

When Laurel visits—every other weekend now—Greta insists on serving meals in the dining room and culls flowers from the garden, roses for the table, a bud vase of freesia for Laurel's room. Greta likes to hear how the remodeling is coming along at the new house, and Laurel feels not constrained but safely held to the easy answer. A few more repairs, just a few. Laurel has heard the tales of the children of Holocaust survivors. Nothing like her family stories. When her mother tells of their escape by boat to the United States, she talks of typing letters to her brother on a typewriter with an *A* key that stuck in the humidity—*we ire going through the Pinimi Cinil todiy.* After Greta and Henry could afford a house with a garden and a second car, they gave to charity every year, luxuriating in the ceremony of discussing where to give their money.

When Abeer interrupts her work to come to the phone, she asks whether the new meds are helping Henry. *Sundowning* is the psychiatric term, the gentle, euphonic name for the half-awake nightmares he experiences, hallucinations of intruders, attackers. Laurel has learned the names of the medications that substitute for the mercy of the gods, Ativan, Paxil, Zyprexa; she has learned how to hold her father's hand warily, closing her fist over his so that he can't crush her fingers in his fierce grip.

Laurel explains to Abeer that she's calling for another reason this time. Over the phone Laurel reads the directions on Mayda's pill bottle. She says, 'Vaginal suppositories. To be taken with food.' What's she supposed to do, shove a ham sandwich in there?

Abeer and Laurel laugh. Mayda sits at the table, waiting.

Abeer explains that the medicine is taken vaginally because it causes nausea, and even then, it's necessary to eat to mitigate the side effects. There are other medications that Mayda might try. Other than aspirin.

When Laurel gets off the phone, Mayda is still waiting.

Yo estoy enojada, Laurel says. *I am angry.*

Mayda looks at her with polite neutrality.

I'm going to find you a better doctor, Laurel says. She tells Mayda that she and Sam will pay for it. What's a neurologist's fee compared to the thousands they are paying every week to the contractor? Laurel calls a referral service to get the name of a doctor who has a translator on his staff and then waits on hold until she can talk to his receptionist, who wants Mayda's date of birth, her Social Security number, her nonexistent insurance information, before she will make an appointment. Mayda doesn't have her Social Security card with her, and she doesn't know the number.

Laurel promises to call back with the required information if the receptionist will *please please* make the appointment now. She has no idea how she got into this, only knows she's a rat trapped in a maze, blindly nosing for the quickest way out.

The receptionist places Laurel on hold again. Twice the line goes dead and Laurel has to call back. When the receptionist puts her on hold for the third time, Laurel starts to cry.

Laurel needed to get to work on time today; it's not strictly necessary for her to be there except for the hours she is in class, but she cannot grade papers at home, amid the noise, without a desk. She hears Mayda moving around in the bedroom, swiping the dust-cloaked furniture, stepping over the tools the contractors have left on the floor. Mayda is not crying.

WINDOW-SHOPPING

Laurel makes an anxious escape from the house every morning, hoping she won't be held back by questions about rebar and wood trim, but when she arrives at work she spends an hour or more reading the spam e-mail that the university sends to all the faculty—job listings, memos on budget planning, and missives from the fledgling part-time faculty union, decrying the status of lecturers as migrant labor. Laurel notes a full-time job listing in the admissions office. She should do something about getting a real job. Last week she and Sam signed the papers on a second mortgage so they will be able to continue writing checks to the construction company. Checks for five thousand dollars. Ten thousand. Twelve thousand.

On Tuesdays and Thursdays, when her four office-mates are all on campus, Laurel is entitled to the office for just a few hours and she wastes them like this. And she still can't work at home. Today, after she dispatches a few students during office hours—but she cares about them, wills herself to inhabit that heroic sense of mission so necessary to her job—she heads for the nearby shopping mall. She gets coffee in the food court and sits at a table to grade papers. Drift beckons her until she gets up, her briefcase on her shoulder, and begins to wander.

She has never paid attention before to the sweet cunning of selling, how displays are arranged to please the eye with such excess of attention. In the women's section of the department store, someone has inserted shirts into jackets on hangers, tacked on the matching skirt below, and pinned the jacket sleeve so the elbow is crooked. A complete composition, with subtle echoes in the shades of color, crisp geometries in the carefully pressed fabric, a promise of ease in the implicit gesture of the creased sleeve. The furniture department is a series of tableaus in which the same loving attention has been paid to complementary hues and tones of color, balanced composition, contrasts in line and texture. Even the careful placement of pillows and vases and fake books and knickknacks suggests, like the clothes, the chance to inhabit this carefully articulated world.

Laurel notes the small mistakes in these arrangements—the slips of taste betrayed in gilt-framed mirrors or gaudy chandeliers or too-yellow pine chests with ball feet—mentally correcting them or thinking of how she might improve on this detail or that. Again and again her slow, slow pleasure is pricked by these flickers of annoyance.

The living room and dining room are the only intact rooms at home, crowded with furniture cleared from the dismantled rooms at the back of the house. Emma does homework at the dining room table, but Nathan sits cross-legged on the sofa with his textbooks and papers spread out on the sofa and floor and shrugs when his homework goes missing. It's not his fault they moved to this dump. Sam consoles Laurel: Nathan is at an age when he's supposed to be disappointed with everyone in the world and particularly with the two people who did the most to con him that things would always be nice. But why can't Nathan manage the simple tasks of an easy childhood and why didn't Laurel suspect something indolent in his even temper? Maybe she has failed to hold up her end of the deal. She can shake with spite just because her boy dodges her kisses. Sometimes Laurel hesitates to accept an embrace from Emma, who still curls against her easily.

Laurel will manage to grade the papers. She's discovered that she can whip through them. She has a series of numbered sentences in her head, as strictly memorized as her mental record of all those tableaus in the stores, and she only has to skim-read and then arrange her written comments: #3, #8, #14. Her students don't notice, just as Sam doesn't notice how much later she comes home on Tuesdays and Thursdays. Her life doesn't seem to require her presence. She can murmur soothingly when Emma wants to talk about a book she's reading, spar with Nathan (arrange the sentences: #4, #2, #1), nod at a friend with a faintly anxious look that mimics attention. When all the while she's thinking about whether the Klee print above the mantel in their living room should be hung a few inches lower or the blooming orchid moved from the bookshelf to the painted Moroccan chest.

WALLOWING

At 10:00 P.M. Laurel sits on the front steps, waiting for a twenty-four-hour plumber to arrive. The only toilet, which her family shares with the construction crew, has backed up for the third time since they moved in. It's a school night, so Laurel must intercept the plumber before he rings the bell and wakes the kids. Sam had to drive to a gas station to call the plumber from a pay phone. Their phone lines have gone dead, also for the third time. What if Greta needs to reach them? Tomorrow Laurel will have to shop for a cell phone, and Sam will have to take a day off to wait for a telephone repairman again. Maybe this time the repairman will fix the phone line so that it doesn't pick up a radio station in the background. Their house seems to generate its own peculiar entropy: when Laurel first used the dryer, she pulled out socks so shorn of fabric they looked like tiny nets; the dishwasher scoured the glaze off their plates and chipped the coffee mugs; vegetables rot in the rusted-out fridge, which sweats beads of water that have to be wiped up daily.

The mess from the backed-up toilet soaked a shirt Nathan had left on the floor. Laurel, on her knees, mopping the tile with disinfectant, asked Nathan if next time maybe he'd take the trouble to toss his clothes in the hamper.

Nathan stood over her, watching her work. OK, he said. I'll never throw my shirt on the floor. And the toilet will never break again.

Do you think I have enough to deal with right now? Laurel said. She couldn't keep a teary waver from her voice.

You're so weak, Nathan said.

Laurel wishes she could remain here on these steps, never to be disturbed by the plumber's arrival or by any other want, never to have to go back into the house to clean up after him, to do the next thing and the next thing that living requires, never to be aroused if she can possibly avoid it. She is disinterested in these petty travails, this conspiracy of their possessions. She envies Nathan's triumphant certainty when it comes to cause and effect. Moments don't form a cord, a sequence, and if they cluster, it's more along the lines of bubbles colliding in soapy water. Only accident makes Laurel remember now the way that Nathan, at five, used to make up songs and insist Laurel write them down, leaning against Laurel to watch her put the words on paper. Only random association fires the next memory, neurological neighbor, another moment of a child leaning against a warm adult body, Laurel standing between her father's knees, begging for the pleasure of rolling a cigarette for him. Some power in him translated each of his habits—even one picked up because of lean times—into ritual. She loved dipping her fingers into the pouch of tobacco, sprinkling the thready bits onto the thin sheet of paper, imitating her father's proficiency at rolling it into a tight cylinder. He even let her swipe her tongue across the paper to seal it for him. The sweet smell of raw tobacco was transformed into the bitter odor of smoke once he lit the cigarette. Her eyes watered but she stayed there, inside that cloud of scent with him.

DUCT TAPE

Yesterday it rained, and the newly finished back wall of the house began to leak in the basement. Water streamed beneath the replaced baseboards onto the new concrete flooring. The foreman had to rip open the Sheetrock to search for the cause of the leak. Sam has gone to work, his turn to be on time today, and Laurel has stayed behind for this morning's demonstration. The foreman shows her the possible sources of trouble—a pipe that exits through the back wall, the upper corner of a newly installed window—and promises her that mildew will not grow on that damp Sheetrock when he seals it back up.

In bed last night Laurel and Sam tried to calculate the number of days of delay the leak might cause: the Sheetrock would have to be replaced again; the window seal or the roof might require further repairs; the crew would have to postpone applying stucco to the wall until it was watertight. Too dizzying to translate this into dollars, divided over the coming weeks of work, the coming years of paying off their debt. Sam wondered if they knew someone else who could afford Mayda on Tuesdays. Not yet, Laurel said.

While they talked business, Laurel and Sam touched one another in an indefinite way. Sometimes the newest trouble provoked desire.

I feel like such a rube, Sam said. We manage to buy the only house in San Francisco that will never be worth all the money we're spending on it.

The Bermuda Triangle of San Francisco real estate, Laurel said.

I was thinking we should call in a priest, Sam said. His hand traced delicate arcs on Laurel's skin. For an exorcism.

Laurel felt as if she had the flu, eyes and ears and nose stuffed up, sensory intake at a dim, blurry minimum. But she managed to follow through on what was expected, with a faint awareness that at least Sam might have some pleasure.

When the foreman releases her, with confident promises, Laurel goes up to the kitchen to find Mayda scrubbing the cupboard beneath the sink. Mayda motions for Laurel to come and look. Water has pooled at the bottom of the cupboard, a thin film that might go unnoticed if Mayda weren't so thorough in her work. Mayda rearranges knickknacks when she dusts, aligns books on their shelves, adjusts pictures on the walls, devotes scrupulous attention to the field in which she can apply her intelligence.

Mayda catches her lower lip beneath her teeth. She apologizes as if this is her fault. She taps the cold, dewy drain pipes for the sink, guessing the cause. Where the pipes form a trap beneath the sink, an S-curve, they are jointed together, and Laurel feels along these joints but discovers nothing definite.

You are supposed to fix things when they break. Right away. But this leak is minor, small potatoes compared to the wall. Laurel kneels with her hands pressed between her knees and stares into the cupboard. Mayda gets to her feet and says something, a flurry of Spanish that Laurel seems to have forgotten how to decipher.

Her father has forgotten how to eat. He has not lost the habit of appetite. He sits down at the table, pleased with what's before him: toast softened with butter and cut into cubes, scrambled eggs, applesauce, cottage cheese. He can't manipulate silverware but is ashamed to be fed, so he pushes food onto a spoon with a fingertip and hauls it shakily to his mouth. He salts his cereal, or drops sugar cubes into his coffee cup until it overflows, or fumbles for a napkin when one is tucked beneath his chin like a bib, performing a life's small rituals with no remnant of intent. Each morsel of food, so slowly harvested, he tucks away in his cheek. Eventually he chokes, coughs, gags and gags.

Laurel's mother purees chicken and broccoli and makes sauces to cloak the fact that this is baby food. Gives Henry a butter knife so he can believe he is cutting his meat. Weighs him every day to record his steady losses. Leaves the house only to go to the grocery store. Laughs with Henry when she's getting him dressed in the morning, buttoning and tucking.

Mayda comes back with a roll of duct tape. She wipes the pipes dry with a rag and then begins to wrap them with the tape. Laurel remembers that this is her problem, after all, and reaches in beneath the sink to help Mayda pull the roll around the pipes. When they have finished, Mayda turns to Laurel with a worried expression on her face.

What can Laurel do about that? But Mayda's expression reminds her to ask if Mayda brought her Social Security number with her today, so Laurel can call and confirm her appointment with the neurologist.

Mi esposo se dice, no molesta usted, Mayda says.

No molesta. Mayda's deliberately simplified coda whenever she asks for anything, her requests protectively translated into mere nuisance. Through the narrow conduit of their shared vocabulary she and Laurel manage to communicate what neither can literally understand and to hover, always, on some margin of misinterpretation. Laurel has to intuit what Mayda wants to tell her, hazard the right angles of another maze: Mayda's husband doesn't want to bother Laurel, which means they should cancel the appointment with the neurologist, which means—maybe—that Laurel overstepped some boundary line in making the offer in the first place, or that Mayda needed time to concoct the polite excuse of her husband in response to Laurel's (paternalistic?) gesture, or that Mayda's husband sensibly vetoed this plan because Mayda *did* get caught—momentarily—between her own wish for a sweeping solution and what experience has surely taught her, to apply duct tape.

TWENTY MILLIGRAMS, TWICE A DAY

At her annual checkup Laurel learns from her gynecologist that she is perimenopausal. Crying jags, insomnia that eats at sleep from both ends, lethargy—all can be chalked up to physiological causes for which Laurel bears no responsibility.

Since she's a good doctor, the gynecologist always tries to check in on how Laurel's life is going. Laurel mentions the house, the disruption of her work (which is only part-time), the fact that she has been spending alternate weekends in Los Angeles, visiting with her mother and her dying father. The gynecologist nods. The normal stresses of middle age, she says.

At last! The causal chain Laurel has been searching for. Causes, once declared, predicate solutions: Switch from the pop radio stations to NPR. Wear an estrogen patch. Get a job (the real kind, where people earn promotions for working hard). Take a weekend for yourself.

Laurel takes a weekend in Los Angeles: When she arrives at her parents' house, she finds her father in his armchair, a wheelchair parked beside him. The attendant her mother hired sits with him, here to bathe Henry after dinner and sit beside him during the night so Greta can get some sleep. Her father doesn't recognize Laurel, but he's sure she is someone who loves him, and he gives her a kiss. They sit together, holding hands, and he points at light playing on the wall and asks Laurel if she can see who is there. No one listens to him, he's tried to warn them, but no one listens. He clenches his fingers within Laurel's; she has to maneuver so that her hand remains over his. Once he gets a grip, he can't let go, only squeezes tighter and tighter. He starts to count out loud, multiplying numbers, faster and faster. Laurel pulls the curtains so he won't see the shadows cast by the light, and he quiets. He classifies the people that he knows, trying to determine who is number one, or two, or three, or four. Listening to him is like reading a poem: Laurel has to make an intuitive leap to interpret the fragments of language she is given. He lists his grandchildren, both number one, and his own only child, naming Laurel to herself, and then laughs and names Greta, Greta of course. He considers whether a particular friend is number one or number two, mutters something in German. He shakes his head. We don't know anyone who's number four or five.

Laurel needs the attendant's help to lift her father out of his armchair and into his wheelchair so he can be wheeled to the bath. Held upright, he wavers; he can't make his left leg move backward. He looks down at it with an expression of judgmental doubt Laurel knows so well; he has never bothered to explain when Laurel did something he thought of as foolish.

Laurel coaxes him. Can I help you lift your left leg to get it behind you?

He emits a grunt of amused exasperation. Bribery, he says.

On Sunday when Laurel gets home, Nathan wants help with a paper on *Twelfth Night*. At first they riff on all the wonderful epithets in Shakespeare: Go *shake your ears, you time-pleaser, you affectioned ass, you passy measures pavin.* Then Nathan refuses all of Laurel's advice, keeps protesting, But what should I *say?* Laurel walks away from him, and Nathan slams his bedroom door, opens it and slams it again, setting loose a shuddering cloud of construction dust.

When Laurel goes to check on him, she finds the window open and Nathan gone. Sam says he's probably just snuck out to the yard. It's nine o'clock at night. Laurel can't keep hold, even for a few hours, even through such ordinary tests, of her patience, when in her father's presence she was so conscious of it as gift, promise, invocation.

Nathan is not in the yard. Laurel gets in the car and cruises the streets of the neighborhood to look for him, forced to drive slowly as she scans the sidewalk. After fifteen minutes, Laurel's heart begins to pound; she's arrived by such slow increments at her destination, the panic Nathan seems determined to lead her toward, as if it's some truth Laurel has spent her whole life evading.

When Laurel finally spots Nathan on a corner, coatless and hunched against the cold, she flips on her brights, forcing Nathan to shield his eyes.

She pulls up beside him and rolls down the window to talk to him. I could be a child molester, Laurel says. Get in the car.

No.

Laurel slams her hand on the horn, and Nathan jumps.

You are a horrible person, Nathan says. He turns his back on Laurel.

Laurel is forced to drive along behind him at a crawl. What is she supposed to do, tail him for the rest of his life? No impulse to tenderness could breach the rampart of her son's braced arms, his furious knowledge: what good is it to be held if you can't be held forever?

Here's what Laurel can hold in the palm of her hand, a foil packet in which are set small oval pills, pink as Easter eggs. A sample packet the gynecologist gave her. Paxil. What her father takes, crushed and stirred into a bowl of melted vanilla ice cream. The symptoms of perimenopause could just as easily be symptoms of depression. Laurel can take these pills if she wants to. Not to erase suffering, which is perpetuated by causes outside the body, so much as to correct a chemical misfiring in the brain, called—something else.

COSMOLOGY

Laurel makes sandwiches for dinner. Today the gas company turned off their gas, so she can't cook. A blessing in disguise: she doesn't like to cook anymore, has forgotten how to pull it off, forgotten the vanity that used to make her labor for hours over boneless chicken breasts stuffed with goat cheese and jalapeño peppers, veal osso bucco, glazed Cornish hens. She could have ignored that smell on the other side of the wall from the stove, dismissed it as paranoid hallucination. She could have talked herself out of believing that she smelled gas and therefore never called the gas company and initiated a process bound to confirm the malignancy of her attention. Washing lettuce, she sternly directs herself not to think about the taped pipes beneath the sink, not to direct any psychic energy there.

When Sam comes home, he heads straight for Laurel in the kitchen.

OK, Laurel says. You're supposed to say, 'Hi, honey, how was your day?'

Oh no, Sam says.

Oh yes, Laurel says. The guy from the gas company came out and shut off the gas—no stove, no heat, no hot water. There's a leak. They're very strict when it comes to fire hazards.

This is like the story of Job, Sam says. Only the bowdlerized version.

Oh sweetie, Laurel says. It gets better. The foreman was here when the gas guy came, and he was so nice. He found a plumber who could come today to check out the gas pipes. I canceled my office hours at school so I could wait for him. The plumber shows up and pokes around under the stairs where all the pipes connect to the main pipe. And he comes and gets me and he has this long look on his face.

Laurel has to stop to laugh. Sam laughs with her, even though he has yet to hear the punch line. She tells him, The plumber wanted me to see the problem for myself. He sprayed water on the pipes and then he forced pressurized air through them, and the water was bubbling at every joint. He'll have to replace the gas pipes in the house. All of them.

Hissing the news of multiple leaks. The thrill was so close to pleasure: poison had been seeping into the air while Laurel's family slept unaware. Laurel's voice shook when she asked the plumber if he could start the work soon (and for what price), and yet there was something so wonderful about this next lesson in the physical properties of things, the self-evident clarity of his proof.

Sam says, Did you know that in the Middle Ages, they used to punish sinners by penning them up with geese? It's really possible to be pecked to death.

You're making that up.

Sam shrugs. It's only little things. But I'm beginning to think the universe is conspiring against us.

Laurel decides not to introduce him to the alternative: some other mysterious glitch, lately discovered in the wiring inside her.

If only it were true, she says. At least then we'd get to feel important.

NONE OF THE ABOVE

Laurel makes Mayda's coffee, stirs in two teaspoons of sugar, and then sits with her at the table to chat. She asks Mayda if she is still having headaches, and Mayda says the new medicine is better. Laurel guesses she must have gotten another prescription from the clinic at the county hospital. Mayda says she has trouble sleeping, but Laurel isn't sure if this is because of the tumor or the medication. Laurel says that she has trouble sleeping too.

From somewhere below them, there's a thud as a carpenter hammers at the wall, and Laurel flinches. She cannot get used to the construction noise, the sound of blows raining down as men rebuild her house. The gods have poor aim too. There are only these bungled missives that may or may not encode ruin. Or maybe it's that Laurel misjudges the peripheral cues she's given. The kind of peripheral cues—*right turn after the yellow house, second left after the light, there's the bus stop*—she is forced to rely on when she tries to talk with Mayda, nothing ever precisely located. There's just stumbling on. Even when Laurel tries with Nathan, summons her son's exact words—Do you really think I'm a horrible person?—the best she can get for an answer is an annoyance she has to guess is regret: You *know* that's not what I meant.

Mayda is telling Laurel something about her parents' house in Oaxaca. Something about how hot it is there. And a machine she wants to buy here and send home.

Air conditioner, Laurel prompts, and Mayda shrugs and nods.

Mayda apologizes for her poor English. *No sé.* She doesn't know why she can't learn the language after living here for twelve years. She and Laurel watch each other's faces and hands, listen so carefully for inflection, the nuance words won't grant them. The way Laurel listens to her father.

Mayda says she did not mean to stay in this country when she first came. She wishes she could go home to Mexico.

Yes, Laurel says, and she knows just what Mayda means, just what reason she wants to give for her failure to learn.

Laurel struggles to construct a sentence. Porque su corazón es rosa.

Because your heart is pink.

Mayda has to correct Laurel. Triste. Su corazón es triste.

Those Who Walk During the Day

Those who walk during the day do not stumble,
because they see the light of this world.

—JOHN 11:9

Because of the rain Timothy unlocks the church doors a few minutes early, keys chiming on the huge ring he takes from his pocket. The men enter single file to check in for the night, each of them burdened like a mule with his worldly goods, some humped beneath heavy backpacks, others struggling to compress their possessions into the span of their arms. Dripping from the rain, they bring with them an awakened cloud of dismay, the rank smell of unwashed bodies, the remnant odors of liquor, cigarettes, stale piss. Stink accompanies them like an insinuation, like something Timothy might train himself not to register. He waits for his body's objection to subside.

At the check-in table the men hand over social-service chits to the staff and open their bags for inspection. The shelter has only three rules: no drugs, no weapons, no pets. But despite their latex gloves, the church workers get nervous about poking into the filthy mess inside the bags. In the nights when he is locked in the church basement with the men, Timothy has seen them use on each other paring knives whetted to a razor sharpness, bottle openers that can churn through skin, belt buckles filed to a point. Some of them can't face the twelve hours without a fix.

Timothy doesn't hesitate to poke a bare hand into a duffel bag or answer a protest with a clap on the back. These men are his vocation. He foundered, but he discovered it. For eight years now he has worked to be ready to receive the goodness in them. Like cautiously cupping your hands over a moth that's gotten into the house, feeling the astonishingly faint tremor of its wings before you release it outside. He has thought often of Paul's promise in the letter to the Romans: And they will be upheld, for the Lord is able to make them stand.

Timothy spots Michael in the line, his nylon sleeping bag rolled up bunchily and held awkwardly under one arm. Only the slightest quivering betrays the contraband wrapped inside.

Timothy circles toward Michael, careful not to block his path. Barely 5'9" and wiry in a way that anticipates the spry old man he'll be in another ten or twelve years, Timothy avoids even a hint of physical threat, just as he holds back from testifying to these men, who can only be drawn to Jesus by the mute attentiveness of deeds.

He says, You know it's against the rules.

Bud's too sick to make any trouble, Michael says. He can't even stand.

The dog has been dying for weeks. A fist-sized tumor protrudes from beneath his ribs; his eyes are gauzed by pus; he suffers seizures that leave him snarling and snapping. Michael carries him everywhere now (thirty pounds or more of dead weight), feeds him watered-down baby formula with an eyedropper, and keeps trying to sneak him into the shelter for the night, only to end up on the street with him.

The dog's head emerges from the bag, and when Michael cups its muzzle in his hand, the dog shudders with worshipful pleasure.

Michael grins. He don't know beautiful from ugly.

Timothy can't allow Michael even to tie up the dog in the church's interior courtyard. They'd have almost as many dogs here as men if he did that.

You could leave him under the bushes out front, Timothy says. If you don't mind drying out the bag after, he'd be all right wrapped up like that.

Mess with me, Michael says, and I'll make you sorry.

Michael is one of the ones who wake up at three in the morning and curl their bodies into a fist, waiting for dawn and release.

To an addict, kindness is a weakness. Timothy says, Those are the rules.

The man standing behind Michael prods him. Quit holding up the line.

Timothy's wife has taught him a little trick for saying no to people who can't bear to hear it. As a nurse Martha gets plenty of practice dealing with people in extremity. She says you never say no outright but offer them a choice, let them come up with an answer even when only one is possible.

You can step out of line to think it over, Timothy says.

He ought to wait—if Michael decides to leave, someone has to make sure the doors are locked again behind him—but he also needs to check on the kitchen. Responsibility for buying the food and cooking the dinners rotates among a number of congregations in San Francisco, in two-week shifts, and every night Timothy supervises volunteers who must be taught the intricacies of the church's unreliable ovens and shown how to stir cornbread mix in metal bowls the size of bushel baskets. Every night he starts over with a new crew of people who don't understand why he fusses about how they set the tables or the way they slice the homemade desserts they have brought with them. (Portions must be equal, or men will agonize over which to choose. They crave sugar, especially the addicts.)

The volunteers in the kitchen are rosy-cheeked and sweat-slick from the heat of the ovens and the steam rising from the cooking pots. Timothy goes over the checklist with the woman who's heading up the crew, and he curtly rejects her notion of setting tangerines and leaves on each table as a centerpiece. It's only human for the volunteers to be so eager to please the men. And still he is annoyed by the way this woman ticks off items on her fingers, by the blond highlights in her hair and the bib apron she has brought from home.

She reminds him of his ex-wife, that's why. Neat, trim, tasteful, everything you could want in a corporate wife. He smiles at the woman, relieved to absolve her.

It's only because Jan called today. Every time she calls—and in ten years, and with the three kids between them, that averages roughly twice a month—he feels a remnant shame for striking the blow she has never understood. She doesn't throw it up to him—that wouldn't be nice—but she treats him as if he is mildly deranged.

As if she has to be wary even when she imparts good news. That's it. That's why. Jan called to tell him their daughter was getting married. To that nice boy she brought out to meet her father last summer. Jan sounded out Timothy with a skittish caution: would he be willing to come, or would he want her to let Susan down gently; would it be all right with him so long as it was some kind of church wedding; would he be uncomfortable if they served alcohol, maybe only wine. When he was pleased for Susan. Pleased for Jan, who was looking forward to planning the wedding.

If he were a normal father, his daughter would have called him herself. He was the one who had quit their life. Had surrendered to Jan the money and the house and the kids and kept a car so he could pack a few things and drive to the coast and start over. Because he couldn't go on like that, sixty-hour work weeks and expense lunches and bleary business trips, salesman of the year three years running, and coming home to the kids sprawled in front of the TV, not even looking up to register his arrival, and spending an entire Saturday with Jan choosing tile for the kitchen they were remodeling again because they had to do something with their income. It wasn't a life most people would have run from, but the profound emptiness Timothy felt — either you put a gun in your mouth or you accepted Jesus into your heart.

This too his ex-wife would — must — regard as mild affliction, ordinary existence apparently just too much for him, and treat with such a painful tact, circling it the way she skirted the matter of money, hoping they could swing a live band instead of a DJ, offer something better than a chicken dinner.

What does a wedding cost these days? Timothy said.

I know you don't have much, Jan said. But even a simple wedding will run upwards of ten thousand dollars.

He didn't have any savings. He'd meant to forswear the burden of accumulation when he left everything to Jan; he'd never expected to marry again, risk another failure. But Martha didn't mind that he made so little money running the shelter, and she was an elder in the church, like him. He'd started a small pension account, and he supposed he could scavenge from that.

He told Jan he could give four thousand. He didn't tell her where the money would come from. She was happy, and he hadn't heard her sound happy since they'd lost their middle child. That second sundering blow.

Timothy helps carry food out to the dining room, where men already wait in line. The volunteers ladle beef stew onto the paper plates the men hold out, scoop salad in amounts Timothy was careful to specify. The men thank the servers, or ask for more potatoes and less meat in their portion of stew, or murmur that the food sure smells good, their courtesy eliciting smiles, questions, a joke or two. Not all of them and not any of them all of the time can do this, but it is how they approach grace.

Timothy moves among the tables, stopping to talk to men he knows or to introduce himself to those he doesn't. They talk about basketball (Timothy culls tidbits from the sports page every day), the weather, the food tonight and how it is or isn't like a meal they remember having somewhere else, and sometimes Timothy shares another tale of Martha's sorry efforts to cook, roasting a lamb till the meat fell off the bone or forgetting to dip the chicken pieces in beaten egg before she rolled them in bread crumbs. Martha would not mind.

When Timothy sees Michael at a table, he can't help imagining the man weighing his own hunger against the dog's misery, concluding he could do nothing for him anyway.

He can't help imagining that choice, the one you never finish making. So many years in which he could do nothing for Jan. And then today the jubilation in her voice. The shock of it, to hear her talk about the price of a wedding gown and how important it was to serve a sit-down meal and do the flowers right.

When Timothy squeezes his shoulder, Michael balls his hands into fists. His knuckles are scarred by scratch marks and scabbed-over puncture wounds left by the dog's teeth. He says, Your charity ain't worth shit.

Grace is not the same thing as ease. Those first few years after Timothy left his family, consciousness of having sinned against them took the shape of a brute physical suffering: tremors, migraines, a gnawing sourness in his stomach. He shook in the presence of his children when they came for a court-ordered visit. God had granted him a new language, and yet he did not even make his children say grace at the table, balked at forcing this on them too. When Timothy got the call from Jan, he made her repeat every detail of the car accident—who Nicky was with, where they were going, what the other driver said when the police arrived. None of it was information he needed. He lay down in bed, still gripping the phone, listening to Jan while his body vainly sought the shape of his son's. Nicky had lain in this bed all day on his last visit, curled in the blankets, saying he was too bored to get up. Timothy had let him stay in bed, afraid to pry, ashamed to inflict his longing on his son. His consciousness of sin had itself been a sin. The sin of despair.

Timothy gets himself a plate of food. There's an empty chair at Michael's table, but he hesitates. He should never hesitate.

When Timothy takes his seat across from Michael, Brian and Antoine are arguing. About whether animals can see in color or not. Brian claims that humans are practically color-blind compared to birds and fish.

Antoine says, What you talk this kind of nonsense for? You ask Preacher Man here. Man the king of this paltry world, and all them animals and birds and fishes made for his use.

Timothy's Idaho-bred ears have trouble with the rolling vowels of the old black men and the smacked consonants of the Asian immigrants. But he has no trouble understanding the debates that flourish at mealtime, the hunger to solicit belief from another person overriding any appeal to logic.

He offers the expected quote from Genesis. And let them have dominion over the fish of the sea, and over the fowl of the air, and over the cattle, and over all the earth.

Thass my man, Antoine says.

Michael grunts.

There's a little tiny shrimp, Brian says, the manta shrimp, can see something like three times more colors in the spectrum than a human.

Antoine folds his arms across his chest. What for? he says. Shrimp ain't even got a brain. Ain't nothing but a spinal cord and a teeny little tube of shit.

But that's the beauty of creation, Timothy says. All the things that amaze us, beyond any purpose.

You *betray* me, Antoine howls.

Well, finally, Michael says. It takes a moment for Timothy to realize he's being addressed. You spit out something don't come out of some rulebook.

Timothy is spared having to answer him, because Brian and Antoine run right over the interruption, Brian saying something about cones in the eyes that process color, Antoine answering that it's his one complaint, they never get ice cream here. From there they jump to the shortcomings of the city's new ballpark—no more cheap seats.

Rarely do the men talk about the life they live now, not even to complain of their accumulation of ailments, the arthritic knees so many of the junkies get from jumping out windows time and again (impulse that seems to govern their drug euphoria the way that flying recurs in everyone's dreams), the swollen, gangrenous feet of the diabetics, the dry mouth that is a side effect of lithium. Later in the evening Brian or Antoine or even Michael might confide to Timothy about a lost family or a stint in prison, but even these confidences are churned up like so much flotsam. It's not possible for most of them to tell a whole story and not necessary: all of them have ruin behind them. Like him.

He wakes in the morning to marvel at the elation of loving Jesus. Yet sometimes he still feels as if he is walking in a dark house, bumping into things that seem to loom at him out of the pitch black, things whose positions he ought to have memorized. Sometimes—now—things seem to be bumping into *him*: Nicky filling an empty soda bottle with vinegar and baking soda and snapping a balloon over the mouth of the bottle so the mysterious gases would make it expand, a magic trick, a miracle. Susan crying on the first day of her first visit to him after the divorce and refusing to say why and finally whispering that she'd gotten her period and needed him to take her to the drugstore. Trevor pulling the two younger ones in a red wagon, though maybe it was a photograph Timothy remembered and not the actual event. Jan putting on lipstick in the car on their way to some party, shimmery smear, and she always did it without the aid of a mirror and puckered her lips as if for a kiss when she finished. Jan doing the same thing in the church vestibule before they went in, side by side, to sit through Nicky's funeral service.

Things that can't occupy the same space at the same time but do. Today she'd called him to rejoice.

After dessert the men have another hour before they have to bed down. A few of them gather at a table where a man plays chess with a teenage volunteer, offering teasing advice to the girl, who grins and blushes as if they're flirting with her. Such a sweetness for them.

The smell of smoke filters in through the door to the enclosed courtyard, where men huddle under the shallow overhang so their cigarettes won't be extinguished by the rain. Timothy will harass the guys only if they fail to pick up their butts. Michael stands among the men outside, both hands shoved in his pockets, shoulders squared as if he is enjoying the bracing effect of that cold rain splattering from the overhang. Slowly he moves out into the rain to peer into the bushes that flank one wall of the courtyard, and then he ducks back to shelter.

He must have smuggled in the dog. Someone must have helped him. To evict Michael, Timothy would have to call a cop, a procedural caution. But he can find an option short of absolute declaration and shy of making an exception: for tonight, at least, he can avoid confirming his suspicion.

He checks on the volunteers in the kitchen; their enthusiasm wanes when it comes time to scrub the huge blackened pots. Next he checks the washrooms. The parishioners have proved tolerant when it comes to the wear and tear on the building, the occasional thefts from the kitchen, but they rebel at discovering in the washrooms evidence of their night tenants, a crust of vomit on the sink or filthy rags or toilet seats speckled with piss.

And every night someone tries to sneak the chance to wash up. In the women's room Timothy finds a young man, stripped to his BVDS, foot up on the rim of the sink as he shaves his lathered leg. He is barely more than a boy, scrawny-chested, his eyes outlined with eyeliner.

For the razor too Timothy should call a cop. Then this kid would have to go out and earn himself a place to sleep with those velvet-rimmed eyes, those sleek legs.

If you let me have that razor, Timothy says, I'll give it back to you in the morning.

Timothy holds still. The man sets the razor on the rim of the sink, flecks soap from his leg, and yanks his pants from the floor to step into them, both hands practically occupied, giving Timothy the chance to pocket the razor. Later he'll have to come back to clean the sink of soap scum and clotted hair, but his priority now is to back out the door.

Martha is right. You must always leave a desperate person room in which to move. Three days and three nights he spent with Jan when he came home for Nicky's funeral. He had to call on Jesus to help him through every minute of it and he could not console her with that truth. She needed him instead to hold her while she wept, to endure it when she pounded his arms and chest in rage, to force himself to stay awake those nights she could not sleep, to grind his jaw in order to keep silent when she accused him. *Three years was all we had left with him, and you had to have your Jesus.* By the day of the funeral his neck and arms ached so much that he winced when she leaned on him at the cemetery, dug her nails into his arms as if her pain could be relieved in this transference. Who was he to promise her that she too could stand in the light?

Timothy returns to the kitchen to dismiss the volunteers, to check their victorious sense of accomplishment by reminding them to wipe the steel counters with bleach or replace the condiment baskets in the correct cupboard. Then he has to go out into the rain and tell the smokers to finish their last cigarette and come inside so he can lock the door. He is patient, and in return they swallow resentment, tap the keys on his ring on their way inside and ask him which one is the key to the kingdom of heaven.

When Timothy stands at the top of the basement stairs to wave the guys down, he makes sure that Malcolm, who always wants to go first so he can have a cot by the heating vent, is granted this privilege before he starts a fight. Malcolm is in his sixties and has been coming here for years, and he is quietly cooperative in all else.

They have another hour before lights out. The men choose cots, testing mattresses with expert haste, and unspool their things from the bags that passed the search at the door. Timothy takes his place at his desk near the entrance. He opens the filing cabinet with its row of neatly labeled manila folders: Social Security Administration, Veterans Administration, methadone clinics, AIDS treatment programs, mental health clinics, halfway houses. Every night men sit down to fill in a form or to hunch beside Timothy as they dictate information. Every night at least a few of them decide they will seek assistance or get off the street, and every morning after they have gone, a janitor fishes forgotten forms from beneath the cots.

Brian keeps wetting the pencil with his tongue as he fills out the application for the AIDS treatment program, which rejects homeless men unless they're living in detox or shelters.

They don't take all their pills when they're on the street, and if they skip doses, the virus becomes more resistant. Smitty just wants a stamp so he can write a letter to his sister in Denver, and Timothy peels one from the wrinkled sheet in his wallet and sneaks it to him across the desk. The church can't afford to supply stamps, and Timothy's own budget will stretch only to one sheet of stamps a week. Seven dollars and change, and the phone bill is never more than thirty dollars a month, and he and Martha wear long underwear to bed so they can keep the utility bill down in winter, and that four-thousand-dollar check he must write to Jan is beyond the scale of his economies.

Jerome takes his place in the chair beside Timothy's desk and says he needs to reapply for disability.

He holds up his right hand, missing the last two fingers. I ever tell you how this happened? I used to be a commercial fisherman up there in Alaska. Man, that was some life. When the fish were running, you'd go out and set nets and haul forty-eight hours straight without sleeping. And it's light just about twenty-four hours a day, and every time you pull in a net, you got these big fish thrashing, and their scales flake off on the deck like glitter. Caught my hand in the gear wheel when we were pulling in a net, and no one could hear me over the motor. And the guy owned the boat, I thought he was my friend, but he claimed I was drunk when I got my hand caught, and I couldn't collect workmen's comp.

Timothy knows just how long to listen, so the line won't stall and so that Jerome will get his chance to tell somebody. Just as he knows not to hope and not to be disappointed. Jesus exists in the now. When Paul wrote to remind his converts of the sweet aroma of the risen Christ, he was naming something witnesses had measured with their senses, the clean scent of a body that did not decay. A recent, literal event.

Jerome pulls a kinked bit of twine from his pocket so he can demonstrate how to tie a nautical knot, and Timothy thinks, teach me again, Lord.

When there is no longer a line before his desk, Timothy tucks away all the paperwork. If he has time later he will start a letter to his daughter, telling her how proud he is that she has arrived at this beautiful moment of her life. But the bills must come first. He and Martha have ordered their days carefully because they have to: her shift is from 3:00 to 11:00 P.M. at the hospital, his is from 6:00 P.M. to 4:00 A.M. here, and even their sleep overlaps by only a few hours. Martha cleans house before he gets up and he runs errands after he walks her to work and does the bills here. If he sleeps no more than seven hours, they can have lunch together, a tiny bit of private time. Enough.

When he tells Martha about Susan's wedding, she will not leap to worry whether or not she should come and how Timothy should greet all those in-laws and former friends who will treat him with a stiff formality at best. She will not needle him like Jan does. Even after seven years Jan will still sometimes start to cry on the phone, rage with a grief that can't still be fresh, expect him to stay on the line until she has cried herself out, tempting him to share her despair, as if only some flaw in him could account for his silence.

But do not presume to teach others. Only one teacher, and Timothy turns to Him every night once his chores are done, reading the Bible by the light of his desk lamp. It takes him three weeks to read the New Testament, start to finish, and then he might dip into Isaiah or the Psalms before he starts over again.

Always he is moved by the story of Jesus, who snapped at His mother when she came to Him at the wedding in Canaan, doubted His Father in His final hour, wept with the sisters of Lazarus, grieving for their brother despite His promise that they need not fear death. A faltering Savior, taking on all the errors of human nature, not at all like the God of the Old Testament, whose wrath was perfect and unassailable.

At lights-out, Timothy counts heads: fifty chits collected at the door, so every bed must be occupied. But one bed is empty, which means he must search for whoever is missing. Best guess, it's Michael. Hiding in the courtyard with that dog because Timothy forgot to hunt for him before lockup.

Timothy grabs the ring of keys and heads up the stairs to unlock first that door and then the door to the courtyard. Michael and the dog huddle beneath the overhang, dimly haloed by the single bulb in the light fixture above them.

Timothy slips outside. He shivers, thinks of how cold his house will be when he goes home at the end of the shift and slips into bed beside Martha, sleeping with a knit cap pulled over her ears, knotted in the blankets so tightly he will have to yank to free a share for himself. She will roll over and murmur something sweet that counters her body's hoarding of warmth. In her easy way she will help him find a way to pay for a good suit for the wedding, so he won't shame his daughter yet again, among the flowers and garlands and perfume.

Timothy beckons to Michael. Come inside. I don't want to have to evict you.

Michael folds himself over the dog in his arms. Bud snarls and snaps, and Michael curses him and hammers his muzzle with his fist.

Even in the poor light Timothy can see that the dog's teeth have scored fresh slashes on Michael's knuckles.

He's a misery to himself, Timothy says.

I ain't worth shit to no one but him.

Michael tightens his grip on the dog, but it fights free and disappears into the bushes, tunneling its way beneath the prickly barrier of branches.

I got a whole can of Similac in him tonight, Michael says. That's more appetite than he's had for weeks.

Michael gets down on all fours to sweep an arm beneath the bushes. Only the rustling of the branches gives away the dog's determined effort to escape.

Enough. Timothy will go inside and call for a cop. No hurry, whenever a patrol car is in the vicinity. He'll contact Animal Control.

He tells Michael, It would be a mercy to put him down.

Michael plunges an arm deep into the bushes, locks his fingers on something, and tugs. The bushes shudder furiously, and Michael writhes in pain, adding his howls to those of the dog.

The two of them roll on the ground, and Timothy steps out into the rain to put a stop to this. He reaches into that moving darkness, furious roil, and gets hold of the dog by the back of its neck, but Michael roars No! and slams his elbow into Timothy's face. Timothy loses his grip, and something razor sharp scrapes along his forearm, furrowing skin.

Timothy can't tell the rake of the dog's nails from the slash of its teeth on his arms, can't tell the man's blows from the dog's, can't separate out the sources of the seeping miasma of foul breath and wet fur. He has no choice but to swing his own fists and not care which mark they hit, and he's in it and of them, a single blundering beast.

Radiant beast, which can devour the instinct to recoil.

When Michael and the dog roll away from Timothy, release comes as a shock, abrupt and intolerable severance. If not for the pain firing up in Timothy's arms, he would feel bereft.

Michael pins the dog to the cement, pressing his elbow against its neck until the dog holds still.

The dog whimpers and lifts its head to lick Michael's hand.

Michael begins to weep in hoarse gasps. I ain't worth shit.

For so long Timothy has steeled himself to listen to someone cry. The slash marks on his arms keep burning, his nerves straining to impart devastating news. He could open his mouth and let the rain pour down his gullet and fill him. He could open his mouth and curse like Michael at the frailty of this vessel.

He could open his mouth.

You're valuable to God, he says.

Michael hauls the limp dog into his arms for another crushing embrace.

Wicked Stepmother

Lexie had not spoken to her mother since before her trip. Amanda had sent packages from Greece—delivered nearly every other week, in huge cartons that were eerily weightless, stuffed with padding to protect the fragile gift at their core—but these did not count as communication. Her mother could breach a bulwark Lexie had spent four months erecting simply by calling to announce she was home. I'm at loose ends again, she said. After she broke up with a man, Amanda always looked around for her mislaid children. Lexie should come for dinner as soon as her mother got settled, and was she still working at the animal shelter? Still? Amanda would put her in touch with a few of her contacts.

Her mother, it seemed, had not noticed Lexie's silence. So did it count? This question took up Lexie's next session of therapy with Nan. Now, of course, she wanted to see her mother, hurl at her feet this proof of continued negligence.

Well, Nan said, you must not be finished with her.

I promised myself I would hang up on her if she called, Lexie said. I didn't. I said I liked working with animals.

Her mother had not lost her touch while she was away: *Oh, honestly. Rescuing poor orphaned puppies. Every adolescent girl's fantasy.*

Like I'm making it all up, Lexie said to Nan. And I start to believe her.

When Lexie tried to remember being Amanda's teenaged daughter, she called up the image of herself at thirteen, relegated to the kitchen of another rented vacation house, begging a plate of food from the serving staff while a party went on all night long, going up to her room to discover one of the guests in her bed and making her way through the strange house to find where her mother might have put her brother so she could crawl into bed with him. *Wicked stepmother,* they said, postulating how and when this woman had been substituted for the real mother they deserved. J.D. was two years older than Lexie and a son, and not until she was fifteen or so, when he would toss her a blanket and insist she sleep on the floor, did she catch on to his amusement.

Lexie had spent her twenties attempting and reattempting college, studying dance, taking up pottery, getting her heart broken with regularity and without any of the increase in judgment you might expect in consolation. Another game, and wasn't it lucky that her exasperated mother could afford to insulate her from harm. When Lexie turned thirty, she started therapy. She learned to think of her monthly trust check as hush money. Resolved to stop dating for a while. Found a steady job. Paid all her expenses, except for therapy, from her salary. For six whole months.

When you first came to see me, Nan said, you told me you were flooded with pain. How does it feel *physically* to imagine being with your mother?

Like I've only just managed to get my feet under me, Lexie said.

That's progress, Nan said. You're not drowning.

Lexie had a recurring dream that she was building a boat. The dream began with Lexie standing in a frame just large enough to hold her, its wood braces curved like ribs. Nailing planks to the hull, she reveled in real pleasures, from the weighted hammer head that made a fulcrum of her wrist to the metal taste of nails in her mouth and the gloating progress of her hands over a smooth slab of wood. With pitch, she caulked the infinitesimal seams between one board and the next.

Nan encouraged her to explore this metaphor: A ship was a *she*. Launched in celebration. Built in hope of survival. Like Noah building the ark to escape the Flood.

J.D. reached Lexie at the adoption desk of the animal shelter. She wasn't answering her phone at home; her mother might call.

He wanted to know if he was interrupting her at anything important.

Lexie looked at the puppy in her lap. Left all day in the cages at the back of the office, puppies were less likely to make a successful adoption. Dogs for whom a home could not be found were eventually put down.

I'm socializing a puppy, she said.

You spend too much time in therapy.

There's a study that showed the more mother rats held and licked their babies, the more confident the babies were when they grew up.

How exactly do you tell if a rat feels confident?

I don't know, Lexie said. They do better at mazes or something.

J.D. said, She wants you to come to dinner Sunday. Just you and me.

He knew Lexie could not afford to come within her mother's orbit. Of course it did not make sense that Lexie went without a car because she couldn't budget for insurance, but if she preferred hiring a limousine service when she needed to get to the airport, she could charge it to Amanda's account.

The puppy began to gnaw on Lexie's finger, and she clamped his muzzle shut. All he needed to understand was that it bothered *him* to nip her hands, and all it took to teach him was consistent repetition.

Lexie had a real job to do here, devising fund-raising campaigns, strategizing the best locations for sidewalk adoption sites. Still, when she punched her time card or filled in at the adoption desk, she felt like a tourist. A sophisticated tourist alert to the transient surprises that travel could bring. Something would come of this that she didn't yet see. Look what she'd culled from last year's trip to Indonesia with her boyfriend. They'd stumbled across a funeral procession on the island of Sulawesi. Six men carrying a coffin built in the same shape as the Torajan houses, *tongkonan*, narrow dwellings with roofs that curved sharply upward at both ends to mimic the prow and stern of a boat. On an island a coffin would need to be shaped like a boat, built to glide across a treacherous, unknown sea.

Lexie said, She doesn't even know I'm not talking to her.

Where are we going with this? J.D. said. You want her to lick you all over? Because she's not that kind of a rat.

Lexie envied him. He'd earned a degree in philosophy from Princeton in the requisite four years, and then he'd come home and started a bookstore with seed money from their mother. Maybe he'd been cutting into his slender profit margin lately by collecting rare books and first editions, but he functioned smoothly.

I know that, Lexie said. You never want to admit that I get it.

She's always so much nicer when she's between men, J.D. said. Are you going to let that go to waste?

She's so much nicer, Lexie said. Remember how she used to let us sleep in her bed sometimes, and we thought it was such a treat? Only when no man was available. Only when she was lonely.

The bitch! J.D. said.

Even Lexie preferred to fetch from the cage a puppy rather than an older dog, whose flaws had already assumed some intransigent shape—cowering when you put out a hand, or yapping, or reflexively lifting its lips from its teeth as if to snarl.

Do you know I've gone five months without a boyfriend? Lexie said.

Wow, J.D. said. That's almost as long as any of them has ever lasted. Who holds the record on that, you or me? Is it six months? Seven?

The thing with Cal was serious. We even went looking for land together.

Oh, yeah, he wanted to get an organic farm going in Mendocino. And you boned up on the evils of pesticides. You sure make the most of your few months with them.

Rounding out my education. What've you got to show for all *your* boys?

Lexie forgot. She started to have fun, and she forgot. For a while she and J.D., both boyfriend-less, had kept a weekly date for the midnight drag show at Trannyshack, where they watched Donna LaDiva, in perfect makeup and a sheer slip dress, lip synch to Judy Garland *and* Laurie Anderson. J.D. said it was very postmodern, that blithe shift from the helpless gestures of the retro female to the stridency of a dominatrix. Just a toss-up, which way you leaned. Silly. Not beautiful. Not brave.

Lexie was eight when her father died. She had been bewildered by her mother's explanation, by the memorial service, by J.D.'s sudden irritation with her. She hadn't known her father was going to go away, or she would have prepared for it, the way she did when her parents took a trip, filching an earring from her mother, a handkerchief of her father's, the shaving brush from his toiletry kit. A few months after the funeral, when her mother was packing for a solo trip, Lexie got careless and took from the suitcase a drawstring pouch her mother used for packing shoes. Amanda discovered the stash under Lexie's bed—the pouch, a pair of nylons, the sash to her silk robe, a cigar stub Lexie had pilfered from an ashtray just before her father died. Amanda gripped her by the elbow and swatted her once, soundly, on the rump.

That's the only time she ever hit me, Lexie told Nan. But I couldn't stop. I took things from her boyfriends when they slept over. I'd wrap this stuff in Kleenex and shove it in my backpack and throw it out at school. I got better at covering my tracks.

What did you take? Nan wanted to know.

A wallet photo. A concert ticket. A key, swiftly threaded free of a keychain.

Was that really so careful? Nan said.

Nan asked leading questions when Lexie was describing her boat too. It was just of a size to hold her? And the curved frame made her think of ribs? As if Lexie had to be guided to the obvious conclusion. She was constructing a womb.

Before dinner Amanda served drinks in the living room, where the huge picture window offered a panoramic view of the bay, spectacular at sunset, with the rounded hills of Marin hunched at the horizon, the span of the Golden Gate Bridge gleaming copper in the fading light, the cargo ships moving so imperceptibly on the water that the few sailboats still out seemed to dart and zip like gnats around them.

Lexie had come to prove to J.D. that she wouldn't cross her arms and glare at her mother across the table: *I'm not talking to you!* But Sunday dinner would be a catered meal for seventeen, with Lexie's place at the table designated by a name card, like everyone else's. A waiter hired for the party had answered the door to her, and when she came up the stairs—three flights, but she never took the elevator—her mother merely waved at her from across the room.

Not a flicker of surprise at Lexie's shorn hair. Lexie had commanded the hairdresser at Supercuts to take it all off: yes, like a buzz cut. For twelve dollars, well within her budget, she'd found a shortcut to the simplicity her mother cultivated at such expense—a single jewel at her throat, a sleeveless dress that bared the firm curves of a woman exempt from aging, hair tinted and layered to look as if someone had just run a hand through it.

Like their mother, J.D. moved as if conscious of the pleasure he gave, only he was so tall he stood out in any crowd, and the colt-like skittishness of his gestures made him seem a creature apart. He at least came to fetch Lexie and deliver her to a woman who served on a hospital board with Amanda. Stooping a little to whisper in her ear, J.D. told Lexie, Mom invited her just for you.

The psychiatrist was a serious woman who could not manage small talk, and pretty soon she and Lexie were discussing the new generation of antidepressants. Lexie protested Carol's belief in their miraculous efficacy. She had tried them for three months—steady weight gain and no more orgasms, and how could you be happy at that price?

Carol was recommending Lexie try Celexa when Amanda joined them, a hand hovering at Carol's shoulder.

You know, everyone's taking happy pills, Amanda said. On my flight home, the woman in the seat next to me offered me a Zoloft, said it would help me sleep. She kept insisting I should take one. What is the polite thing to say to that?

They were joined by a man whom Lexie's mother introduced as her partner in crime. She and Roger were allies on some civic improvement project.

When he discovered Carol's profession, Roger wanted her advice too. He and his wife had agreed to let their teenaged daughter bring her boyfriend along when they went up to their house in Tahoe for the weekend. The kids had gone upstairs to his daughter's room while he and his wife packed the car, and once they were ready to leave, he hollered for his daughter. When she didn't come, he went to fetch the kids and opened the door on the two of them, buck naked, going at it.

Amanda threw up her hands. What is the polite thing to say?

Well, Roger said, they were downstairs five minutes later, fully clothed, and we drove for three hours in absolute silence. And I just don't know—what should I say to my daughter? How personal should I get about this?

Carol said, You should apologize for opening the door without knocking.

Amanda played with the tangled chains strung on Lexie's neck—a locket, a Buddhist medal, charms on a beaded string, what she privately sighed over as tribal tacky. Her touch called up nights Lexie had shared her mother's bed, squeamish and thrilled. Amanda's flirting had an automatic and androgynous quality, as if everyone who came within range must be seduced, but only up to a certain point, short of any consequence. Lexie had trouble believing her mother actually slept with any of the men she dated.

Amanda said, I did a lot of things wrong, but I always knocked on the door and waited to be invited in.

You ought to have burst in once in a while, Lexie said.

Carol and Roger laughed.

Amanda said, There's your answer, Roger. Damned if you do, damned if you don't.

At least there had been no Snow White dilemmas for Lexie: her mother had not, as might have been predicted, competed with her once she grew tall and willowy herself. At fifteen she had sex for the first time in her room upstairs, with a stable hand from the barn where she took riding lessons, an immigrant from Romania who barely spoke English. Lexie had sneaked off with him on a Sunday afternoon and then, plagued by guilt, taken him home to introduce him to her mother. Amanda invited him to dinner and made no objection when Lexie took him up to her room. Where he jumped her, angrily rooting at her body for something she couldn't see, speaking words that could have been a hand at her throat: he loved her, he wanted her to have his baby. Only in relating this story to Nan had Lexie understood that she'd brought him home so her mother could protect her.

When Lexie had to go off antidepressants, Nan promised that talk therapy altered the brain's chemistry too, as mysteriously and effectively as the drugs. You could will some alteration in the firing of nerve cells, concede that the synapses constituted an ephemeral reservoir of the self.

Lexie caught her mother's hand. You haven't said one thing about my hair.

It's so playful, Amanda said. I could never get away with that. Your brother has been scolding me about giving up the blond highlights. At my age.

J.D. reappeared on cue. It's true, he said. It's time to stop living under false pretenses.

Amanda rolled her eyes. I take so much abuse from my children.

If J.D. could pull it off, so could Lexie. She said cheerily, And I thought it was the other way around.

Amanda turned to Carol confidingly. Lexie's my sensitive one. Some children just are. When she was a little girl, she was terrified of our elevator. She wouldn't get on it. And then I'd catch her in the hall, pushing the button to call it, making the doors open and close, open and close, over and over.

Lexie went to the bar to order another drink. She spent the rest of the cocktail hour flirting with the caterer's bartender.

She knew what she was doing. Contriving affinity out of all that time she'd spent as a child in the kitchen with the servants, which was not—oh, poor orphan—merely a craving for shelter. After the Romanian stable hand, she had slept with one of the ever-changing crew of young men who weeded and pruned her mother's garden. A handyman or two. Her mother's yoga instructor. None of them quite so dirty as the stable hand, whose declarations she'd deserved, because in the real world where Lexie went looking for him, you paid for things. There was another truth that had escaped Nan.

When the bartender asked for her number, Lexie dug an eyeliner pencil from her purse to write on a cocktail napkin. She folded it into a tiny square to tuck in his shirt pocket, creasing the napkin with her thumb, over and over, until she'd smeared the penciled numbers into a watercolor blur. Postmodern. Undecipherable.

It was weak of Lexie to agree to go shoe shopping with her mother, to accept this substitute for the cozy family dinner her mother had promised but failed to deliver. They visited a number of stores for a little avaricious looking and then retraced their steps and got serious. If her mother could not recall any of Lexie's boyfriends (and Lexie could always name hers—Steve, this last time), she had a talent for choosing just the right gift, had found in Greece tiny decanters of translucent pink glass, clouded with age, that would make perfect candleholders for Lexie. Amanda had the salesgirl bring out one pair after another of gorgeous shoes and wanted Lexie to take them all. But you could try them on only one pair at a time, and each time you might balk. Lexie paced back and forth, trying to decide if the sexy open-toed red heels pinched her feet or if she had any use for them.

Shoe shopping was weirdly akin to therapy. In both cases you banged smack into the predicament of sex: Lexie asking her mother, Can I actually walk in these things? and her mother answering, Who cares? They're for swooning in; Lexie confessing to Nan that when she was a little girl, she thought only some people had nipples, not everyone, and Nan answering, Have you thought about whether you want something from men that you can't get? In both cases the perfect fit mattered as much as it had for Cinderella: An eight-and-a-half or a nine in this pair? Had Amanda been too withholding or too careless in her bursts of affection? In both cases you relied on someone who encouraged you to buy or to cry: Go ahead! You're entitled! In both cases a beautiful proliferation would have to be checked by choice.

One invitation led to another, with Lexie agreeing to go up to Calistoga with her mother for some girl time, only to discover J.D. was coming with them, and then working through with Nan her feeling of being second-best, which she ought to have, set beside her beautiful centaur brother whose company would be as enticing for her as for her mother. She wanted to know if she was disappointing Nan. Nan wanted to know if Lexie was asking *her* to make the decision.

After they checked into the hotel for the weekend, the three of them went to the mud baths. Lexie and her mother parted with J.D. at the door of the changing room, where they showered and were handed thick terry-cloth robes and led out to private tubs by a lab-coated attendant. Lexie glimpsed her mother naked for a moment before she sank into the mud—the unlined perfect body of a woman who could live practically on air, never eating more than a single meal a day. Now that her mother was without makeup, Lexie could see a faint rash rimming her jawline and stippling her cheeks, but when she asked, her mother refused to explain, as if Lexie were compounding the insult to her vanity by noticing this flaw.

Lexie had never tried the mud baths before, and she had worried she might not like sinking into that thick gooey mess. But her body was surprisingly buoyant in the mud. It yielded to your weight just a little and then nosed at you like a dog, a timid exploration, reminding her of mornings at work when she'd go into a cage of puppies to fetch one to bring back to her desk, and the puppies would coalesce around her, blindly stepping on one another as they strove to arrive at her, all their insistence blunted to the soft, tentative contact of nose or tongue.

Lexie and J.D. split two bottles of wine over dinner. Amanda had never skipped a cocktail hour in her life, but she said she wasn't feeling quite right and refused to join them. J.D. crowed about snagging a first edition of *A Farewell to Arms*. He'd had to buy six cartons of books in order not to alert the seller to the one treasure among them. He'd thrown out most of the books, but at the table he produced something he'd salvaged for Lexie.

Lexie opened the book to find incomprehensible diagrams of sailors' knots. He'd remembered her dream about the boat. The dream had begun to make her feel claustrophobic: something hovered just beyond its parameters, tiring her out. Couldn't she quit dreaming now? she had asked Nan. And Nan had reiterated the obvious: It's the means for leaving your family, leaving behind its traumas and its hurtful patterns. Everyone has to do it, even when things haven't been so bad.

Speaking of tying the knot, Amanda said, I am so excited that our new mayor decided to marry any gay couple that applies for a license. Short-lived, maybe, but a lovely gesture. J.D., will you be sending out invitations any time soon?

Sweetheart, J.D. said, why would you assume I had any more interest than you in that bourgeois institution?

I pulled it off once, Amanda said.

She raised a hand to her cheek as if to scratch and then returned it to her lap. Her foundation makeup had been smeared on thick as cream.

Lexie asked her mother again for a reason. What gave you that nasty rash?

Steve sent lilies, her mother said. Baskets and baskets of them. It was a gentlemanly gesture. A way to say that it was good while it lasted.

Amanda was very allergic. Lilies had to be removed immediately from any flower arrangements that arrived at the house, bagged in plastic before they could shed their pollen, and taken out to the trash.

Lexie drained her wineglass. You must have told him.

I guess he forgot, Amanda said.

Maybe you should see a doctor, Lexie said.

Amanda shrugged. I'm taking Benadryl.

It looks worse than it did this afternoon, Lexie said.

You don't want to nag, Amanda said. We're having such a good time.

The rash must explain why her mother had forgone her usual weekend parties to spend time alone with her children. Or it explained why she hungered for the comfort of their company. Or the comfort of their company was so tenuous a thing that at any moment it could be demolished by Lexie's fickle sensitivities, or it was her mother who was fickle, inviting her children into her bed and then kicking them out as soon as one cold little foot found her warm skin.

Amanda tapped Lexie's wrist. Don't pout, sweetheart.

I'm not *pouting*, Lexie said.

J.D. said, Let's all go back to your room, dearie mum, and get into our sweats and watch a movie.

Amanda said, oh, yes!—when did she ever allow herself just to be a slob?—and after J.D. and Lexie left her at her door, with promises to return as soon as they'd changed, Lexie asked him why. Why was he always switching the subject just in the nick of time? Why must he compulsively douse all fires?

Swaying a little, he gave her a smacking kiss on the top of her head. Someone's got to look out for you.

Once all three of them had gotten into sweats, they settled on watching a kung fu movie dubbed into English. Amanda, who would never admit her craving for shoddy fare, had found reasons to reject all other options. Lexie sat beside her mother on the bed, both of them with their feet straight out in front of them, quilted cotton pads folded between each toe. J.D. had made only a pro forma protest—of course you want your fairy son to paint your nails—before he set to work, first on her mother, and now on Lexie.

Things were not so bad, things were again as amicable as that kiss J.D. had given Lexie in the hall, and still she felt hemmed in, tilted precariously toward Amanda on the mattress, pricked by the rapid-fire voices coming from the TV set, unsettled by J.D. wielding the brush as if its diminutive size alarmed him.

J.D. capped the polish. You know what? We all have a foot fetish.

Amanda wiggled her toes. You could pass for a pro. It's a comfort to know one of you can always find gainful employment.

J.D. sat down heavily on the edge of the bed.

Don't get that look on your face, Amanda warned Lexie. You've really stuck it out at that place. You've earned yourself a little vacation. I'd love to take you with me to Montana next month.

I won't get any time off till I've been there a full year, Lexie said.

You could go back to school, Amanda said. You could train to be a therapist. You're so interested in it.

It's not a *professional* interest, Lexie said.

Certain things should remain unspoken among civilized people, Amanda said. What you do in bed with someone. What goes on in therapy.

Lexie scrambled up from the bed. She stood over Amanda, her fists clenched. You're always trying to buy me off. So I'll never have the guts to tell you. It really, really hurts to be your daughter.

I can't breathe, Amanda said.

Amanda was stealing Lexie's panic attack right out from under her. She screamed at her mother. I haven't been able to breathe for a long time!

My—heart—is—racing, Amanda said.

J.D. pulled Lexie back from the bed. Jesus, Lexie! She means it.

He bent over Amanda. Where does it hurt? Do you have chest pain?

Amanda put a hand on his arm, but she did not speak, only stared at him with a stunned expression.

J.D. reached for the phone on the bedside table and punched 911 and in a level voice gave Amanda's room number to the dispatcher.

Lexie sank onto the bed beside her mother and began to cry.

This time Lexie had screwed up irreparably. This time she had caused her mother to have a heart attack. She cried when the paramedics arrived and pressed a stethoscope to her mother's heart, cried when they offered reassurances but advised a trip to the emergency room, cried as she sat with J.D. in the hospital waiting area. J.D. spoke to her only once, to ask her to please stop that, and she said OK, and he turned to her as if she had offered him an argument. It *is* nicer to take a trip than to go to work, he said.

Two hours later a doctor called them in to see their mother, propped up on a gurney and dressed in a threadbare hospital gown. She had taken too much Benadryl. Vanity had made her reckless, and a drug that caused drowsiness in a normal dosage range could produce heart palpitations and anxiety in the amounts at which she had been downing it.

Another plummeting shift in Lexie's understanding. Another ridiculous toss-up.

As soon as she got back from the trip, Lexie made an emergency appointment. In Nan's office, she tried to describe what it had been like, waiting in the tiny exam room until the doctors were sure Amanda's heart rate had returned to normal.

J.D. and her mother swung right into their routine. J.D. had something to hold over Amanda's head now. Just think, if her friends found out she'd been carted to a hospital, braless and in sweatpants, for taking too much antihistamine.

Honey, Amanda said, you're open to a little blackmail yourself. The nurses had to remove the cotton pads from between my toes.

Amanda glanced at Lexie, seated in a chair against the wall with her mother's purse in her lap. I knew I could count on you to remember my purse, Amanda said.

Some bone had to be thrown.

Crying, Lexie looked up at Nan. I *was* neglected. I didn't just *feel* that way.

Nan passed her a Kleenex. There's a type of therapy in which you simply train the client to change cognitive patterns. You don't worry about insight, so long as you get results.

That's how it's done with dogs, Lexie said.

Nan rarely betrayed surprise, but she did now. Well. It works with addicts too. A person can get hooked on intermittent reinforcement.

So soft and persistent, this lulling guidance.

This is what your dream is telling you, Nan said. You're ready to quit them.

Was that all? When she first learned to read, Lexie had a picture-book Bible in which the ark held a jolly congregation of animals, all paired, all honoring the truce of necessity, the lion with the lamb, the elephant accommodating a snake in its stall, a smiling snake. But the story of the ark had always worried her. In the hasty winnowing the animals could not have been marched two by two up the ramp. Some of them must have surged onto the boat frantic and alone, the last of their kind. So many must have been left behind. Wishing she could reinstate the missing, Lexie had drawn in the margins of the book. Unicorns and dragons and griffins.

Lexie said, Or else it's about my parents not taking me on their trips.

You can make up your mind for yourself, Nan said.

Or else, Lexie said.

But she was afraid to finish. Afraid of the steady supply of affirmations from Nan. Afraid of how, in the blue fluorescent light of the exam room, the hives on Amanda's face had stood out like blisters, and she had looked wan, a momentarily deflated version of the creature who held sway wherever she was domiciled, punctilious about her every preference, from the way a grapefruit half should be sectioned to the ritual of aspirin every night to ward off a hangover. Steve hadn't forgotten her allergies. Lexie sat in the corner and watched them, her mother and her brother who, like her, could not marry, both of them valiant in a way she was not.

After she left Nan's office, Lexie took the bus to the maritime museum at the Hyde Street Pier. For some time she'd been meaning to visit the three-masted sailing ship berthed here. From a placard at the top of the gangplank, she learned the *Balclutha* had been in use from the mid-eighteen hundreds to the nineteen-thirties, carting lumber up and down the coast, over two thousand tons of cargo on each trip. A capacity that seemed impossible, measured against the compactness of everything aboard—the narrow, tiered ledges that served as beds for the sailors, the tiny galley, the steep, ladderlike steps that connected one deck to another.

By putting her hands on the real parts of a ship, its pulleys and blocks, the beveled spokes of the pilot's wheel, a canvas sail rolled tight, would she destroy what was beautiful and mysterious about her dream? Where did it come from in her mind? Why were the planks she nailed into place in her dream as narrow as those on the real ship, and how had she imagined so accurately the caulking tool she used?

When she descended into the hold, Lexie was assailed by the evil smell of mildew, a century of fetid decay suspended in the air. She wanted to turn and flee, but she made herself keep going. Down here, the rocking of the ship was more eerily manifest. Daylight had never invaded this darkness, a seeming infinity that might forever be subdivided—how many thousand tons on how many trips?—but was in fact so small a space. Even this ship reeked of all it could not contain.